Tombstone's Goldmine

The man known only as Tombstone was a pretty tough, resourceful puncher. He would need these qualities to escape the wrath of the ruthless ranch boss Dutch Maxie after he had intervened to save the lives of two young brothers who had fallen foul of the murderous rancher.

Fleeing west, towards the Pacific, Tombstone and his friends are caught up in the gold rush of 1849. Amidst treacherous ambuscades and Indian conflicts, Tombstone encounters and rescues feisty Belle Fair, who has been captured by a war-painted Indian.

Now, their only chance of a future is to face the vengeful pursuers closing in all around them.

Tombstone's Goldmine

Gordon Landsborough

A Black Horse Western

ROBERT HALE · LONDON

© 1951, 2005 Gordon Landsborough
First hardcover edition 2005
Originally published in paperback as
Hombre from Tombstone by Mike M'Cracken

ISBN 0 7090 7703 3

Robert Hale Limited
Clerkenwell House
Clerkenwell Green
London EC1R 0HT

Typeset by
Derek Doyle & Associates, Liverpool.
Printed and bound in Great Britain by
Antony Rowe Limited, Wiltshire

CHAPTER ONE

DUTCH MAXIE

Corny chased the last bacon grease with a hunk of rye bread that he had picked up on the way out, then wiped his fingers on his hair, so as to be able to slick it down. He kicked the fire into a small blaze and then lay back on his blanket.

Next to him lay Rip, his kid brother, legs comfortably crossed, his eyes upon the stars. And in the shadows sprawled the long hulk of the big fellar.

Corny went down at that, a sigh of contentment easing out of him as the soft sand mattressed his lean, hard young body. He too looked at the stars. The night wind blew softly across the mesa, stirring the cottonwoods gently behind them. Somewhere a night bird called plaintively, and far in the distance they heard the low of some maverick cow.

Rip suddenly said, 'To think, last night we slep' on beds.'

Corny said, quickly, 'You sorry, Rip?'

'Me? Hell, no!' Rip was eighteen but he could swear like any man. After a pause he said, 'Yeah, but how 'bout the big fellar?'

Corny rolled on to his side, nose wrinkling doubtfully. The big fellar was still a shadow across the pool of firelight. Corny said, 'Hey, Tombstone, how d'you feel about all this? Reckon we lost you a job today, me an' Rip.'

Tombstone stirred and shoved back his hat. When he spoke his voice was low and good-humoured. 'Reckon you did, at that, you coupla hellcats. Reckon but for you I'd be listening to twenty men snorin' musically right now, back in Dutch Maxie's bunkhouse. Reckon you kinda owe me a lot.'

But the way the big fellar said it, the kids knew that he didn't mean it. Corny said, 'You're a pretty right guy, bud. I figger you got us outa plenty trouble, back there. Me, I aim to make it up to you, an' I don't mean maybe.'

Tombstone said, 'Aw, shucks, kids, that wasn't anything. Reckon I kinda enjoyed myself at that.'

He had. He lay back again, his eyes also looking up at the stars. He thought, 'This is a hull lot better'n bein' in a stuffy bunkhouse. Reckon I'd been there long enough anyway.' Sleeping out on the soft sand under the clean night sky with the cool breeze playing gently on his face – a rough but good meal under his belly, no night-herding, no bawling and stamping and shoving about, like you got at Dutch Maxie's ranch. This was the life.

It had happened so simply, so quickly, that morning. Dutch Maxie had come thumping down from the ranch house, shirt only partly stuffed into his black, store trousers. He was mad. His face was so blue if he'd have bled just then he'd have run ink, thought Tombstone, grinning at the memory.

No one liked Maxie. He was a hard man, at a time when all ranch owners had to be hard to survive. For down on that troublesome Mexican border, if you were soft you went under, back in those roaring days of 1849.

Maxie wasn't soft. The trouble was, Maxie was too hard. He drove his men mercilessly, and didn't care how they ended up. He was a killer, the way he ran things. When the big drives came, there was always a fatality or two because of the way Maxie shoved his men along . . . drive a man too long and he gets tired and careless and doesn't see danger from longhorns until it is too late.

But, that morning, something special had got the boss hopping mad. Corny had been saddling up nearest the ranch house, and he'd been first to get the lash.

Maxie had come roaring his head off, shouting his rage. Corny didn't understand, didn't hear a distinguishable word. And not understanding, he started to swing up on to his horse.

Maxie had charged up, shouting, 'Geddown, damn yer! No one's gonna leave this ranch until I'm through!'

Then, to make sure, he'd grabbed hold of Corny and pulled him out of his saddle. Corny had crashed pretty heavily on to the ground. That was one big mistake that Dutch Maxie had made. He should have known better than to lay hands on the boy. You couldn't touch Corny without inviting action from Rip, the kid brother.

Maxie's right leg was in mid-air, his big mouth opened in a roar of fury, when Rip hit him. Rip drove in, head down, and knocked the wind out of the bull-like ranchman. Maxie hit the ground a couple of yards from where Corny still lay.

Tombstone had seen it all, and he knew what was bound to come. He came flying, heels first, over the top of the hitching rail – a prodigious jump from the raised porch of the bunkhouse. His guns were out and flaming even while he was in mid-air.

Maxie had twisted, the moment he'd hit the ground. The man that laid a hand on the ranchowner didn't live to do it a second time – not if Maxie was in a passion. The kid saw the movement, saw the hand claw out with a sixshooter, and began too late to go for his own.

Corny saw it, too, and shucked his gun, but Tombstone beat them all to it. His blazing guns whipped up dirt in front of the rancher's face and sent him jerking on to his back again. Maxie's gun blatted as his finger involuntarily pressed on the trigger, but they did nothing worse than make holes in the sky.

Then Tombstone jumped the last five yards, feet together, and that brought him alongside the rancher. The big fellar let go with his foot, and Maxie's gun rose into the air and fell a few yards away. The trouble was, Maxie's fingers got in the way, and he howled with pain.

Other men were tumbling out now. Tombstone wheeled; he wasn't taking chances. Maxie had a tough bunch, and he was king over this territory. In those early days they hadn't got around to making laws in those parts, and King Colt, newly invented, settled most disputes.

Tombstone straddled the rancher, his guns waving in threatening little arcs as the punchers started to come near. Particularly he watched the foreman, Jep Shaker, and Alabama George and Kurt Hencken. He knew these three were close to Maxie and would take his side. Some of the other punchers might, too, though not all of them. But Tombstone took no chances. His guns covered the lot.

Maxie shouted, 'By God, you'll suffer for this! Put them guns down!'

Tombstone spoke to him but didn't take his eyes from the group of punchers, standing there, tense and still. He said, 'Like hell I will! And let you shoot the daylights outa me? Tie yore face, Dutch, else you'll get the first bullet outa this hyar Colt.'

Corny had come up behind him, gun in hand, and now

Rip backed into the group, his Colt ready. They stood, three crouching men, Maxie between them, ready to open up at the first movement.

Corny shot out of the corner of his mouth. 'Now, what do we do, Tombstone?' It was the natural thing for them to turn to the big six-footer from Arizona for guidance.

Tombstone said, 'Rip, get our horses fixed, collect our warbags, an' bring some chuck from the cookhouse. We're moving out!' He raised his voice. 'If Rip don't come back within ten minutes, Dutch Maxie's need fer land will have been reduced to a plot six foot by two foot.' He stirred the sullen rancher with his foot. 'Guess you'd better say somp'n to the boys, Dutch.'

Maxie snarled, ' OK! Let the kid get what he wants. But by god you ain't heard the last o' this, Tombstone! I didn't reckon it was you that did it, but seeming it is. But I'll get you if I have to trail you to the Canadian border to meet up with you again. *Nobody crosses Dutch Maxie and gets away with it!*'

Tombstone watched the kid go across to the bunkhouse, and said, agreeably, 'Sure, sure, Maxie. You're a nice kind o' rattlesnake; you don't need to tell me. Mebbe I'd better draw yer pisen now, huh?'

Maxie saw those hard grey eyes come sweeping down to him. They were the eyes of a killer, at that moment, and Maxie went back as if trying to get under the ground. Tombstone was a chilling man when he had his six-gun pointing at you.

But he didn't shoot. Maybe he wasn't a killer without provocation, like Dutch Maxie or his foreman, lean, evil, Jep Shaker. The minutes passed. No one spoke after that. Tombstone and Corny just kept their guns covering the punchers, and no one felt like arguing against those three blue muzzles.

Then Rip came, leading horses for himself and Tombstone – Corny's was still along the hitching rail. He said, 'I got everything aboard,' then swung up and covered the punchers while his comrades climbed into their saddles.

Dutch Maxie got up then, dusting his trousers; his face was black with fury. They spurred their horses back until they were level with the ranch-house corner, their guns unwavering.

Dutch Maxie started to shout, 'You'll regret this—' And then the three whirled their horses and leapt away behind the protection of the 'dobe building. Even so, Jep Shaker got his gun smoking before the last tail disappeared from sight – Tombstone heard the 'plunk' as a lead bullet drove into the dry mud.

The big puncher from Arizona called out to the kids as they lay across the necks of their horses, fanning them with their hats. 'Hey, tie some weights on, younkers. Hold yore hosses!'

They pulled in, then, and he came galloping alongside. 'We got a long way to go, kids,' he grinned. 'An' I reckon Maxie'll have some o' the boys after us, so we'd better not blow our hosses. It'll take time for 'em to saddle up, and that'll give us all the lead we need to keep ahead of 'em.'

He was right. They saw the dust cloud rise way back and knew it for their pursuers, but now they were climbing into the hills west of the Rio Grande and it wasn't hard to shake them off. All day they rode steadily northwards, following an old cattle trail that would eventually come out on the Santa Fe trail. When night came they weren't bothered about the thought of pursuit, and camped openly and comfortably by the side of the trail.

Corny was thinking. 'Hey, Tombstone,' he called. 'Maxie was powerful mad this morning. I've never seen him like that. What d'you reckon had riled the *hombre*? And what did he mean when he said, "I didn't reckon it was you that did it"? Did what?'

Tombstone thought lazily for a while. He didn't feel like exerting his brain. After some moments he stirred and felt for the makings. 'Cain't say why he was so mad. As fer the other part, reckon he was surprised to see who had drawn on him, that's all.'

But Corny shook his head. For a kid of twenty he had an old head on his shoulders. Somehow Tombstone's easy explanation didn't satisfy. He went to sleep thinking, 'There was more to it than just that'.

A couple of days later they made Santa Fe, at the beginning of the trail that led to the rich northland. It was a small 'dobe town that spoke of its Mexican origins, a drab, nondescript place. Normally it was so dull and uneventful that if a dog crossed the dusty main street, people turned to look at it. But this spring day in 1849 was different.

There was a kind of crazed excitement over Santa Fe that day. The town was crowded with people and horses and carts and wagons of all descriptions. Never had they seen the place so busy, and as they rode in they could only wonder at it.

The gambling establishments were packed, and the *cantinas* were gay with song and masculine laughter. In the street were drunks by the dozen.

But it was the people that surprised the three cowboys. In Santa Fe normally you found only cattlemen and punchers, maybe a few teamsters and a sprinkling of smooth gamblers and slick Yankee traders. But this day they seemed to have come from all the Eastern states of America.

There were men from Kentucky, in their fringed buckskin shirts and trousers, coon tails on their caps, and their celebrated long guns in their hands. There were city men from Indiana, Ohio and even farther east – all types of tradesmen, shopkeepers, clerks; and some were near gone with exhaustion and seemed clad only in rags, though others trudged stolidly by afoot and didn't seem distressed.

There were negroes from Missouri, and sharp-bearded planters from Carolina; there were half-breeds and Indians – and there was even a group of sailors who had come in from Charleston.

Cory said. 'What'n tarnation does this amount to?'

Tombstone said, 'I've seen this before. It can mean only one thing.'

Corny said, 'Yeah? Whassat, old timer?'

'A gold strike.'

'A gold strike?' Rip looked round. 'But thar ain't no gold hyar. Silver in Nevaddy, mebbe but . . .'

'We'll soon see,' said Tombstone, and then they began to thread their way through the pushing, trigger-tempered mob that seemed all in a hurry to get somewhere. They came out by the steps of a saloon from which came raucous song. That was where they saw the sailors.

Tombstone leaned down; he had to shout because of the squealing of ungreased wagon wheels and because everyone else was shouting.

'Hey, pardner,' he called. 'Whassall this about? Somebody givin' sump'n away free, huh?'

The sailor, a stocky, resolute man with eyes excited and burning, said, 'It's a gold strike, cap'n. People are makin' millions overnight. We're all off to make our fortunes. How much do you want for yore horse?'

'It ain't fer sale,' said Tombstone equably. 'An' where's this bonanza, pardner? Colorado?'

'Sacramento, California.'

'Holy daisies!' exclaimed Tombstone. 'An' you critters air all off after gold so far away?'

Rip didn't even know where Sacramento was. Corny hazarded a guess. 'It'll be on the Pacific. That's twelve hundred miles from here – twelve hundred of the roughest miles you'll ever find anywhere in the world. These *hombres* must be mad.'

'Wal,' said Rip, 'I reckon there's a lot in the same boat.'

There were. They were streaming through the town by the hundred. Farther along they found themselves wedged in by a couple of high-sided, tall-wheeled freight carts that got tangled with each other. The teamsters got to shouting, then to lashing each other with their whips. Then they got down and closed and went tumbling under the hoofs of their powerful draught horses. The main Santa Fe street was in an uproar.

'They got gold fever all right,' said Tombstone drily. 'Normally all these hellions would stand around an' cheer a scrap like that; now they haven't time fer it – they want to be on their way.'

A tall Kentuckian was on the board walk. His hair was long, and he wore a beard, but his eyes were tolerant and humorous. He was leaning on the four-foot barrel of his long gun, the deadliest weapon then known to the West.

Tombstone said, 'They sure got hot blood in their veins.'

'Sure have,' agreed the Kentuckian. 'Reckon we all got it, me as bad as the rest of 'em. It'll be yore turn any moment now, friend.'

Tombstone laughed and shook his head. 'Not me. Reckon I quit chasing rainbows years back. I ain't stirring myself to go a-chasin' gold jes' because some *hombre*'s seen a streak in a dirt pan.'

The Kentuckian just smiled humorously. 'This ain't no

wild-cat,' he said. 'The government issued a report on the strike, and they opine that it's the richest gold field in the world. That's official, 'cause I seed the report myself.'

'Yeah?' Tombstone's eyes went up. If that was official then it explained everything.

Corny said, 'I ain't never been on a gold rush, an' I ain't got nothing to do. I gotta feeling I'd like to move West. How 'bout you, Tombstone?'

Tombstone grinned. 'Me, I ain't got nothin' ter do, either. But Sacramento's a good thousand miles from hyar, don't fergit.'

Rip said, innocently, 'Is that a long way?'

So Tombstone said, 'OK. Let's all git good an' proper mad an' jine the gold stampede!'

CHAPTER TWO

SCARAMOUCH RAISES TROUBLE

Rip at once started to drive his paint forward. Then he heard Tombstone's lazy drawl, 'You all aim to git to Californy tonight, Rip?' and he drew rein.

'Ain't we startin' right now?' the kid demanded, all hot and excited. 'Ef we waste time, Tombstone, mebbe thar won't be no gold when we get thar.'

'Sure, but don't fergit, son, thar's over a thousand mile o' desert an' mountain to cross. Mebbe we'll git along faster if we start off the right way now. I guess a lot o' these *hombres*'ll jes' decorate the trail with their bones, for that reason – they jes' started rushing out afore they'd got themselves fixed with grub and ammunition and sich-like.'

They always gave way to Tombstone's opinion. He didn't waste words, and for one man he talked a lot of hoss-sense. They drew their horses close to his. Corny said, 'OK, big fellar. You tell us what to do.'

Tombstone was watching the crowded street, especially the slow-moving wagon trains that crawled ceaselessly through the town. He said, 'Thar's the Mohave Desert to cross. Reckon it'd be more comfortable if we crossed it in company.'

'Meanin'?'

'Meaning you c'n carry a bar'l of water on a wagon, but only a bottle on a hoss.'

They didn't understand. He swung down. 'Corny,' he ordered, 'get these hosses outa town. Rip c'n come with me. Make camp back o' the Mex *cantina* where we allus stay on the drives north. We'll be along in about an hour. Oh ... shoot any *hombre* that makes a move fer them hosses. They're worth a man's life, now the gold rush's on, I reckon.'

Corny nodded and rode slowly away along the crowded, noisy street. Rip said, 'Where now, Tombstone?'

The big fellar said, 'I'm gonna hire us out to some wagon train. Mebbe they could do with three fit men.'

Rip said, 'Hell's bells, you ain't gonna take us all the way to Californy behind them slow schooners, air you?'

Tombstone smiled and started to build a cigarette. 'Them slow schooners'll get to Californy, which is more than I c'n say fer a lot of these critters afoot. It's a long way, son, over a thousand miles.'

'But we got hosses?'

'We ain't got money. How're we gonna live in the next two months – because it'll take all that to git to Sacramento? Thar ain't much food on the way, not in the desert part, anyway, an' we'll have no time to hunt fer it.'

Rip said, 'You know best, Tombstone. What you say goes. Reckon mebbe thar'll be a li'l pay dirt left over when we git thar.'

They drifted down the street. After a time they came to a *cantina* where a lot of Eastern tradesmen were doing business. Santa Fe was the end of the trail from the north, and the Yankee traders were unloading their bolts of cloth and barrels of gunpowder and dried food. The prices they were asking were high – they made you jump to see how the cost of things had suddenly gone up since the gold trek started.

Tombstone said, 'Now see how much money we'd need to grubstake us until we got to Californy. An' when we get thar, the prices'll be higher still.'

They shoved their way through to the bar and called for tequilla. Just then an old man came pushing through the noisy throng. He was an old-timer, you could see – spare, mahogany-faced, with keen blue eyes that came from looking across prairies. He had a scrub beard, the kind that comes when you shave once a week or not that often.

He stood on a chair and shouted, 'I got a train I'm taking to Californy. Five wagons. I'll grubstake two or three men that'll ride guard fer me.'

Tombstone said, 'That's us, Rip,' but just then someone called, 'What wages air you payin', pardner?'

The old timer said, 'I can't afford no wages, this trip. But ain't the grub somethin'?'

Someone laughed and said, 'No dice, old timer. We'll be earnin' our second million by the time you come a-rollin' into Sacramento.'

'Yeah?' said Tombstone softly. 'An' mebbe you won't.'

He was going forward, when Rip said, 'Didn't you see who that was, Tombstone? The fellow that asked what wages were paid?'

Tombstone looked now. There was a scrub-faced, mean-eyed *hombre* playing cards, back of the room. As Tombstone watched, the fellar shoved back his hat.

'Scaramouch!' Tombstone said. 'The fellar that lit out from the T-over-X yesterday.'

'Yeah,' said Rip, his eyes getting grim. 'An' he went

17

ridin' out on Corny's saddle, I 'member.' He suddenly gripped the big fellar's arm. 'Look, thar's Corny's saddle down at his feet, right now.'

He started to move over, and the big cowpuncher ranged himself alongside. He hadn't liked Scaramouch – no one had. Scaramouch was a mean *hombre*, and a lazy puncher. When he'd blown, the day before, no one had bewailed the loss, not even Dutch Maxie or his foreman, Jep Shaker.

Suddenly Scaramouch looked up and his eyes met Tombstone's. Somehow they didn't seem to see Rip, as if sight of the big puncher was enough for him.

The cards fell from his hands. Tombstone could have sworn that there was deadly fear suddenly whitening the fellar's skin, and he couldn't understand it. Then Scaramouch shoved back his chair and started to rise . . . Tombstone heard him saying, 'What you come after me for? I ain't done nothin'. You cain't touch me fer somep'n I ain't done!'

It puzzled Tombstone. He'd always known that Scaramouch was without sand, but a fellar didn't take on quite so about another puncher's saddle. His horse, sure – you killed a man for taking your horse. But the saddle . . . Yet Scaramouch was deadly afraid.

Rip stooped casually and picked up the saddle. 'Thanks, pardner,' he said. 'It's kinda old, but it ain't yores,' and he started to walk away with it.

Scaramouch hollered, 'Gimme that back! It ain't yores. I'll buy it from you . . .' And again it didn't make sense to Tombstone.

But Scaramouch made the mistake of grabbing for the saddle and trying to wrest it from the kid's hands. Rip's tight riding boot came up in a swift arc, kicking the fellar's hands away. Scaramouch went for his gun, but the kid, not even bothering to drop the saddle, danced in and kicked him in the stomach and changed his mind about gun-play.

Scaramouch crashed back on to his chair, which broke under him and he fell writhing to the floor. For the next second or two he would be more concerned about getting back his wind than the saddle.

His pardners in the card game didn't look any better than their comrade. One or two started to fiddle with their guns, so Tombstone dropped his hands to his own, and his icy voice crackled out, 'I wouldn't draw if I were you, pardners.' He looked the kind of *hombre* that got vexed if people didn't take his advice, so they abruptly put their hands on the table, to show their good intentions.

A few people started to run for it, in case there was gun play, but the place was so noisy and crowded that the incident had no effect upon the arguing, excited throng only a few yards away.

Tombstone rapped, 'Git goin', Rip,' and Rip shoved his way out, saddle over his shoulder. Tombstone went out – backwards. Scaramouch was getting to his feet now.

They pushed out into the milling throng that surged along the west way of the main Santa Fe street. It was the way the punchers wanted to go, so they got behind a big prairie schooner that was drawn by draught oxen. Behind was another, eight slow, patient beasts pulling the lumbering structure along. After a few minutes Rip felt the hot breath of one of the beasts down his neck, and he turned so as to keep away from the long horns. The oxen wouldn't intentionally harm him, but a fellow could always catch an arm on the points in turning, if they were that close.

Tombstone suddenly found himself being dragged to one side. 'What'n the—?' he began, then realized what was the matter.

Rip said, 'Look, thar's Scaramouch followin' us.

Anyone would think it was *his* saddle, like he said!'

Scaramouch had stopped, his brown breed eyes suddenly apprehensive. Rip snorted. 'I ain't gonna let a *hombre* like that chase me. Hyar, hold that!'

Tombstone suddenly found himself holding the saddle. Rip leapt like lightning and caught Scaramouch before the fellar could turn. Tombstone, from a distance, grinned. Scaramouch was a full-grown man of his own age – nearly thirty – while Rip was only a kid of eighteen. But the kid was a fire-eater; he could hold his own in a scrap . . . as he did now.

Scaramouch snarled and lashed out. Rip came under the flailing arms and ripped into the bigger man's stomach. Then they closed, and next moment the pair went rolling into the roadway, fists and feet going twelve to the dozen.

Instantly there was a commotion – quite a considerable one. The fighting pair went rolling among the feet of the startled oxen, which crescented round across the dusty trail and began to climb through a corn chandler's. They got as far as upsetting some sacks and spilling out the corn and then lost interest in the fight.

The teamster was shouting and cracking his long whip; men from the train came running up to try and keep the wagons moving; and men plodding at the side of the road paused to rest and give encouragement to the contestants. Never was so much confusion started just because two men decided to have a fight in a main street.

Tombstone kept watch for any companions that Scaramouch might have, but none showed. Rip was losing at first because he was the lighter of the two. Then suddenly he clambered to his feet. Scaramouch started to come up, too, but the kid went in, fists hammering with every ounce of weight he'd got.

The ferocity of the attack seemed to unnerve Scaramouch. He started to get away, and stopped fighting back. The kid piled in, bloodying his nose, and opening the *hombre*'s lip for him. Then Scaramouch broke off the engagement. Shamelessly he turned and ran.

An old man on the sidewalk spat brown tobacco stain and said, 'You sure gave that fellar what for, son. You kinda like a fight, don't you, kid?'

Tombstone said, 'The kid's a bully, mister. He's always pickin' on fellars bigger'n hissel'.' To the kid he said. 'Ain't you ashamed o' yoresel', brawling in the street? You'll get a bad name.'

The kid said, 'Big as you are, I'll pin yore ears back if you start sassin' me!'

Tombstone just grinned and slung the saddle over the kid's shoulder. 'Hyar, fire-eater, you c'n carry it fer a change. I held it long enough. Don't know why you bothered about that air old piece o' hoss furniture. Corny's got a better one now.'

'I know,' said the kid, tramping through the dust at his side, the sweat streaming off him following his recent exertion. 'But I 'low I wasn't goin' to let that thievin' varmint keep a-holt on it. He seemed mighty fond of it, at that – Scaramouch, I mean.'

'He sure did,' said Tombstone. 'You know, Scaramouch seemed afraid of us, before we got round to the saddle business. He seemed to me to think we were after him for something. I don't understand at all.'

Rip said, 'Neither do I, and I ain't bothered. Me, I jes' had the dandiest li'l fight, and it makes me feel good.' Tombstone was grinning at the words as they came round to the back of the Mexican 'dobe *cantina*. Back of it was a scrub patch where the punchers used to bed down on one of their nights on the return trail from the northern cattle markets. Corny should be here, waiting with the horses. . . .

Tombstone's hand flattened against Rip's chest and sent him flying against the 'dobe wall. His right hand streaked and found his gun – clawed it out in one swift movement and sent it blazing into the waiting group.

At the same time he was falling, so that the fusillade of bullets passed over his body. His quickness had saved him, that time.

There were five men in the group ... Jep Shaker, Alabama George, Kurt Hencken and two punchers known as Two Thumbs and Sulky. They weren't good *hombres*, especially Two Thumbs who was so called because he had been born without any.

They'd been waiting for the pair to return, that was obvious. They were afoot, their horses staked along with the trio's. Corny was back of the party, covered by the negroid Alabama George.

Because Corny was holding the horses of his brother and Tombstone, they'd guessed that his companions would soon be returning – and they'd been waiting for them.

But now Tombstone was down and rolling into a dry rain galley, and the five surprised punchers were scattering, the tables turned on them by the swiftness of the big puncher's reaction.

Rip didn't waste time. Probably the punchers hadn't seen him at all, because Tombstone had shoved him back before he'd turned the corner. He called, 'Keep their heads down, Tombstone,' and saw the big fellar nod in understanding, and then he went scrambling over a wall and into the *cantina*.

Everyone shot to their feet as the kid came streaking through, gun in hand. It was all right fellars shooting off in the back lot – that was their business – but if the gunning started up in the *cantina*, well, that was their business.

But the kid didn't start anything there. The fat Mexican proprietor was in the way, but the kid just shoved him into a chair, and then started to climb the ladder on to the flat roof where the Mex and his family slept for coolness during the summer.

Out on top he took off his hat, then carefully raised his head to peer over the low 'dobe parapet. The gun battle raged below, and everyone concerned was too intent on slinging lead and keeping out of the way of lead slung back to look up.

The kid saw Alabama George in the background where, the horses tugged restively at their pickets. Alabama wasn't taking part in the gun battle; his job was to look after the horses and their prisoner.

Rip saw that his brother had been forced down on his face; Alabama was sitting across him, one hand exerting an armlock to keep Corny from trying to pitch him off. In the other hand he held a gun – and Rip saw that he was prepared to use it on his brother if the need arose.

The range was distant, but fortunately there would be little chance of hitting his brother. Rip aimed his revolver like a rifle, sighting it carefully and making allowance for drop and wind. If he missed with his first shot, he mightn't get a chance of another, and there was no knowing what Alabama George might do if he heard a shot suddenly screaming mighty close to him.

Rip fired for the chest. Through the smoke he saw Alabama stiffen, half-rise, then topple forward, hands clutching underneath him. Rip stood. up, shouting, 'Get his gun, Corny!' and saw his brother wriggle round in the dry grass and make a grab for the feebly protesting Alabama's hand.

The men looked up at that. Rip saw a white face directly below and opened up. It was Two Thumbs. Two Thumbs went rolling over in agony as lead tore into his shoulder, and Rip smiled a grim smile. He'd often wanted to open up on that varmint!

Tombstone went into action, then Rip saw him, taking advantage of the distraction, hurtle into the open, guns blazing. Sulky went spinning round, hands gripping his side, and Kurt Hencken went back without a sound, a black hole appearing plumb in the middle of his forehead. Only the foreman, thin, mean Jep Shaker was left untouched. He threw down his guns and rose, hands finding large fragmets of sky as quick as they could.

'Hold them guns.' he growled. 'I ain't continuin'!'

'Like hell you're not,' said Tombstone grimly. Then to Rip, above, 'Smart work. kid. Where's Corny?'

'Here I am.' Corny tramped up from back of the scrub lot. 'Alabama's kinda feeling sick. He's sufferin' from lead pisen, I reckon, way he's creatin'.'

Tombstone said, 'What happened?'

'They jumped me.' Corny ran his hands through his brown, tumbled air in disgust. 'I wasn't expectin' it. They must have followed right behind me in the crowd. Soon's I turned off here, they were on to me.'

'What's it about?' asked Tombstone grimly, turning to the foreman. 'It ain't healthy, sticking gun toters up, as you should know. Now, you tell me.'

'You know all right,' growled Jep unpleasantly. 'Maxie sent us after you. He got real mad, the way you went off. You didn't oughta taken that stuff.'

Rip came in on that. 'Wal, the goldarned piker,' said the kid in disgust. 'Trailin' us for a bit o' grub.'

'And a saddle,' Corny reminded him. Rip went back and fetched Corny's old saddle.

'Yeah,' he said. 'And a saddle.' He threw it on to the ground before the foreman. 'We took a saddle because Scaramouch went off with Corny's yesterday, I jes' got it back now. You c'n have it. But thar ain't no need for anyone to get het up at that. Maxie owes us 'bout three week's wages; I reckon that more than covers payment for the grub we took and that saddle. Anyway, thar's a saddle. Give it to Maxie an' tell him I hope it gives him boils.'

Corny said, 'That's my saddle you're givin' away.'

'So what? It ain't no better'n the one you've got on yore hoss right now. I don't reckon to waste any more time here. Let's git moving.'

Tombstone said, 'That's a first-class idea. I never did like to see a lotta blood around the place. Shuck their guns kids, an' let's git goin'.'

A minute later they were mounted and riding away. They turned by the *cantina* wall. They were in time to see Jep Shaker pick the spare saddle up and hurl it as far from him as he could. Then he pitched into his men, bawling them out for not putting up a better show. Sulky said something about Shaker not putting up any great show either, and then they heard no more.

Rip said, 'Jep seems powerful angry,' and grinned. Then Corny said, 'I knew Dutch Maxie was a mean man to cross, but I didn't think he'd send his gun-toters all this way jes' because of that li'l schemozzle.'

Only Tombstone said nothing, riding into the crowded street again. There were a lot of things he couldn't understand. . . .

Corny asked, 'Whar we goin', Tombstone, old hoss?'

The big fellar said, 'I reckon to camp outa town tonight. It's not far to sundown, as it is. Thar's no room hyar in Santa Fe, an' I'd still prefer to bed out again to trying the local breed o' fleas.'

'Me, too.' said Rip. His mind went back to the *cantina* where they'd met Scaramouch. 'Hey, Tombstone, what about that *hombre* with the prairie schooners? You forgotten him?'

But the big Arizonian shook his head. 'Nope. I reckon his train's somewhar ahead, an' we're bound to ketch up with him very soon now. I'd like to see his outfit; if it's friendly, mebbe we'll join him. He'll mebbe need three men with guns, once he gets into Injun territory.'

Now they were leaving Santa Fe and beginning to approach the Grand Canyon. Once out of town the going was considerably easier. Here the trail broadened, so that several streams of traffic could proceed abreast at the same time.

They crossed the canyon, just as night was beginning to fall. Now the trail that led westward began to be pin-pricked with red fires as the gold-prospectors made camp for the night. Only a few fever-bitten men trudged on, trying to get another hour's march in before the light failed and made it impossible.

Big Tombstone watched them go, his head shaking. 'Half of 'em'll never git thar, at that rate,' he prophesied. 'An' when the few do reach Californy, they'll be glad to dig fer other men at a coupla dollars a day. Thar ain't never enough gold to go round on any gold field.'

Then he reined. North a quarter of a mile, way off the track, was a solitary camp. In the failing light the trio just made out five covered wagons, drawn into a loose circle. Tombstone said, 'Mebbe that's the fellar we want ter see,' and turned off the trail.

As they came up a dog ran out, barking. Then someone challenged them from behind a wagon. 'Stand still, strangers. Who air you, an' what d'you want, this time o' night?'

26

Tombstone said, 'I heard a train captain askin' fer men, back in a Santa Fe *cantina*. I'm lookin' fer him. We want to join up, ef the train's not too slow.'

The *hombre*'s manner changed. 'Mebbe at that you'll be right welcome.' Then he shouted, 'Hey, Mark, we got three strangers askin' fer you.'

A few seconds later the spare scrub-faced figure they had seen back in Santa Fe came clambering into view, leaning on a long gun. They didn't take chances with strangers, these pioneers.

The man said, 'Howdy, strangers. I'm Mark Enty, cap'n o' this train. We're aimin' ter settle in the new lands round San Bernardino that the government's offerin'.'

'Thought you'd got the gold fever,' grinned Tombstone, and introduced himself and companions. Enty seemed satisfied and led the way back to the fire in the centre of the wagon ring.

'We ain't gold grubbers,' he said. 'We'd bin plannin' this drive long afore Marshall made his strike and set these crazy folk on the march. We're aimin' to settle an' raise cattle. Southern Californy's a purty good place fer cattle, reports do say.'

Tombstone said, 'I ain't never bin further west than the place they call me after – Tombstone, Arizony.'

'I thought that name warn't natural like,' said the train captain politely. 'Now, what is it you boys want? You look the kind I'd like with me, though the kid's over young . . .

'The kid,' said Rip coldly, 'c'n take care o' hissel'. Don't you git fresh with my age, old timer.'

'Yeah, mebbe I made a mistake at that,' said the old timer, a glint of humour coming to his eye.

Tombstone said, 'You was sayin', back in Santa Fe, you'd grub-stake two-three *hombres* who'd ride an' fight fer you. I reckon yore trail ends south o' whar we intend to go, but

27

it's much in the same direction. Do our faces fit?'

Mark Enty looked at them in the dancing firelight. Around it the women were cooking, and the men were working on harness and wagon gear. He put out his hand at length to Tombstone and said, 'Reckon thar ain't much wrong with what I see, pardner.'

Tombstone had taken a good look round as they came up in the failing light. 'You aim to travel fast, huh?'

Enty said, 'Yeah. We got all horses, no kine. An' with only five wagons, I reckon to stir a breeze some. You'll git along pretty fast with us, mister.'

Tombstone nodded. 'It'll do. Saddles off, boys; here's our new home.'

CHAPTER THREE

THE MAN WHO WATCHED

Their new home was under Mark Enty's wagon when it rained, anywhere out in the open during fine weather. It suited the punchers.

The first night they weren't needed for camp watch, so they had a full night's sleep and woke refreshed. But they were with the first that stirred, and were certainly the first for food when the shout went up that it was ready.

They sat back of the camp on a little, tufty hillock and got outside their breakfast. The sun was just over the eastern horizon, but its rays were already warm to their bodies; the air was clear and exhilarating, giving zest to their meal; in the distance were the blue mountains over which they had to pass, while behind led the bare scar that was the trail leading to the ford across the Grand Canyon.

Tombstone spoke, his mouth full of beans and bacon. He said, 'I wouldn't miss this for the world.'

The two kids stopped eating. Corny's blue eyes turned to look westwards, along the trail they would soon have to take. He said, softly, 'It doesn't seem possible. All that land ahead of us that we've never seen. Well over a thousand miles of almost uninhabited, unexplored country. What an adventure, pards. *I* wouldn't be out of this for anything, either!'

He stood up, luxuriating in the feeling of freedom that had been inspired by Tombstone's quiet words.

'Me, too!' Rip's face glowed. He was still only a kid, for all his fighting ways; and this adventure touched his imagination. 'Wonder what's in store for us, along that trail? Day after day, week after week—'

'Month after month,' said Tombstone. 'Yeah, ef we do it in less than three months, it'll be satisfactory goin' with these heavy wagons. It depends on what we meet on the way.'

'Injuns?' Corny queried quickly.

'Mebbe. Though they shouldn't be so dangerous, with so many of us on the trail. What's a bigger, tougher enemy is old lady Nature herself. Reckon we'll git plenty storms when we git into the hills o' Arizona – and I know what Arizona storms c'n be like. An' then, jes' beyond, you come to the Mohave Desert. I ain't never bin thar, but from all accounts that desert's just one place not to stay too long in.'

Mark Enty came over just then, a smile on his face. He liked the three punchers. 'Ev'rythin' OK?'

'Tol'able,' drawled Tombsone. 'We was jes' speculatin', wonderin' ef we'd made a mistake in leavin' Dutch Maxie an' his dogies. Sech a nice fellar – sech purty dogies.'

Just for a moment Enty didn't realize that the big puncher was joking; then his scrubby face parted in a grin. 'Better be sure now than five hundred miles along the trail,' he nodded. 'Now, you boys will have to take turns in ridin' the wagons, and in goin' off huntin' for somethin' ter fill out the rations. Thar's plenty o' meat way back off the trail, an' someone's gotta keep after it all the time. Jes' one thing. Whoever goes huntin' should watch out for Injuns. Thar's bin a few attacks on small trains lately, I've heerd.'

So they fell into the camp routine. There were eight able-bodied men and youths in the party – apart from Mark Enty and themselves, nine girls and women, and so many children they never quite got their number. The three punchers quickly assumed the role of scouts and hunters by day, and camp riders by night.

Always one of them went ahead down the trail, seeking out the best route for the five prairie schooners. So many wagons had gone this way ahead of them that there was a fairly clearly marked way, but at times they found it easier to cut away from the rutty track and make their own trail.

The other pair rode on either flank, sometimes two or three miles deep into the country. Enty supplied them with long hunting rifles, so that while keeping watch for enemies they also took whatever opportunity they could to shoot game. Tombstone was the most successful hunter, and rare it was that he failed to return with a deer and some birds tied to his saddle.

That was the part that the kids liked best – riding deep into the country off the trail, and foraging for game. Mark Enty was delighted with them. He said, on their second night, 'Looks like you're grub-staking us, not the other way about, friends.'

Tombstone nodded. 'Sure does. But your time'll come. From what I 'member, thar ain't much game in northern Arizona, and thar'll be even less on the plains of Californy when we git thar. It's goin' ter be summer, an' powerful hot by the time we get thar, an' the game keeps outa sight during the daytime.'

Enty nodded soberly. This was no pleasure jaunt, and he knew it. All the time it was going to be a race against water running out, and food supplies proving insufficient for their many hungry mouths. Just now things were all right, but the way they intended to go, Santa Fe was the last town until they reached the Pacific coast of Southern California. As it was, one of their best horses showed signs of going lame, and it would be a tragedy if they were to lose it.

But there was always an hour or two each evening when there was time for relaxation. The punchers weren't used to so many females being about, but there was no doubt that it made for pleasanter evenings around the camp-fire. One or two of the younger girls took a shine for the punchers, but their mothers kept a close eye on them, so that didn't get far.

One night, just as darkness descended Enty came over to Tombstone and whispered, 'Hey, puncher, I want a word with you.'

Tombstone rose and followed. Enty rapped out his corncob on the iron rim of his wagon wheel and said, 'Young Rip's jes' reported somethin' queer. Thar's a fellar bin watching us circle up fer the night from way back among those scrub thorns. Rip spotted him and started up ter meet him, thinkin' mebbe he'd like ter share camp fer the night. But the fellar jes' pulled his boss round an' rode off.'

'Wal?' Tombstone was puzzled.

'Wal, the galoot's back agen. Rip's jes' spotted him hidin' back among the thorns. He's watchin' us.'

'What d'you think, boss?' Tombstone wanted to know what the train captain had in mind.

'I think he ain't no honest man,' snapped Enty. 'Could be he wants ter sneak up an' thieve food, an' powder, an' mebbe a pack hoss. Or mebbe he's got a gang holed up that feel they could do with our wagons and provisions fer the long desert road into Californy. Don't fergit, Tombstone, we're comin' right off the gold trail now; thar ain't many pass so far south as we're doin'.'

Tombstone said, 'Don't alarm the wimmin. But get two or three of your men out on watch. I'm goin' after the *hombre.*'

He saddled up quickly, and saw that his guns were working easily. Enty came running up with a rifle, but Tombstone said, 'That ain't handy, now it's dark. You c'n hold on to Long Tom yerself, boss.'

He walked his horse through the wagon circle, then mounted. Corny was riding watch on the south side; Rip covered the back trail to the north. Tombstone found him in a clump of stunted oaks. The kid said, 'I reckon he's still thar, Tombstone. You wait hyar, an' I'll smoke him out.'

Tombstone said, 'You wait hyar, yer young hellion,' and started to ride past. 'Yore job's ter keep watch an' let no one git near the camp, son, so don't let yerself be lured away. This might be jes' a varmint's trick.'

Tombstone grinned as he heard the kid start cussin' fluently, but he knew that this was a job for someone less impetuous than the eighteen-year-old.

He rode out in a circle, meaning to come up on the watcher from the rear, but either the watcher had grown tired of watching or just about that time something had made him suspicious. Anyway, as Tombstone came softly up towards the thorn bushes, he suddenly heard the crash as a horse was forced through them, and then a dark shadow seemed to leap out towards him.

For one second Tombstone thought it had been deliberate, that the watcher was trying to ride him down. Then he heard the sudden shout of alarm, short and cut off, and knew that the watcher hadn't known he was there.

They weren't more than ten yards apart. Both pulled hard on their horses and sent them rearing and whinnying with fright. Tombstone saw the *hombre* as a dark shadow against the greyer background of bushes. He shouted, 'Hey, you, what're you up to? Hold yer hoss, I wanta talk to you!'

Tombstone saw a red flame flower in the darkness, felt something pluck at the cloth on his sleeve, and simultaneously heard the blat of a six-gun roaring. It seemed to make a tremendous noise in the dark, down here in the scrub-choked gully.

Tombstone kicked his horse round, so as to make himself a more difficult target. His gun was in his hand, but held his fire because his opponent had dissolved into the darkness. Tombstone heard the smack of hoofs on the dry ground, and knew that the watcher had taken to flight.

He pulled his frightened horse round and sent it plunging after the *hombre*. A minute later he stopped.

'Hold yore hoss, Tombstone,' he told himself. 'You're no better'n the kid, harin' off like that. This is suicide, chasing a galoot like this.'

It was. In such a chase, all the advantage was with the pursued and not the pursuer. For one thing, to follow the trail it meant that Tombstone would have to keep halting, so as to be able to hear the other's hoofbeats. That way, halting every half-minute, there was no hope of catching up with the man.

Another thing, mebbe the galoot would only run so far, and then wait until he came up, to pump a stream of lead into him before he knew where he was.

So Tombstone halted and sat in his saddle and listened to the hoofbeats dying away into the distance. He listened, then looked up and marked the way the rider went by the stars. Then he took out his sack of Bull Durham and rolled himself a cigarette, and for the next half hour he sat in his saddle and waited.

Tombstone was no fool. That half-hour was deliberate, designed to throw his opponent off his guard. By now the galoot would be quite sure he was safe, and wouldn't be taking so much care about keeping watch. And, Tombstone had a hunch that he could find the *hombre*.

The way Tombstone looked at it, when a fellar was panicked he just hove straight out for home, without thinking. Tombstone had a hunch that 'home' in this case would be some camp occupied by the watcher's friends.

After half an hour, he rode softly, keeping an eye on the stars and on the way he went. He hadn't gone far – maybe three or four miles – when he began to see a small red gleam off the track to the north.

He turned off and slowly approached. When he was about a hundred yards from the fire he dismounted. From here he would go forward afoot. His cayuse was well-trained and would stand quietly until his return.

Softy he began to approach the fire. Around it he could discern a number of forms – four, five, or even six. But if one was the watcher, he couldn't make out which it was, The wind blew softly in his face, bringing the smell of wood smoke to his nostrils. He heard a horse nicker and then begin to stamp around. One of the men stirred himself, and then strode off into the darkness in the direction of the sounds from the horses.

Tombstone began to inch forward again under cover of the sound. He wanted to get his eyes on to these *hombre*'s faces and see what that might reveal. . . .

The cowboy suddenly went rigid on the ground, and down his spine crept a feeling as if ice had been laid on it. He had detected a soft movement . . . Then he felt something hot breathing into his back. He went rolling on to his back at that, face twisting at the unexpectedness of it.

There was something standing over him, silhouetted against the stars. Something big – gigantic in that faint light. Something far bigger than a man.

The shock of it almost started his guns going. Then he saw what it was . . . understood.

It was his horse. It had followed him quietly, under cover of the sounds from the other horses. Now it was standing right over him.

Tombstone could only stare up through the darkness at his mount. This was something that had never happened before. His was a well trained cowpony; if you told it to stand, it stood without moving even if you were away for an hour or two.

'What'n the tarnation, hoss?' he whispered, and then again he went rigid. Something was biting his cayuse tonight. It was tossing its head, and beginning to paw the ground. Tombstone, lying there, knew that something was exciting it.

For a second he wondered if it was some prowling bear or lion, but then he dismissed the idea. With the fire so close, neither of those animals would be lurking within scenting range of the horse.

He rose quickly, taking a chance on being seen from the fire. He couldn't go any nearer with that darn fool hoss breathing down his neck, so he might just as well lead it away and stake it way back, then maybe try again.

He caught the bridle and started to pull the horse round . . . There was something very curious about his cayuse that night. He could feel the mount resisting, as if not wanting to be led away from the fire.

Suddenly one of the other horses neighed, and immediately his own mount answered the call.

Instantly there was confusion. Tombstone saw men leaping to their feet – saw them as black shadows against the firelight . . . saw the familiar move as hands dived for guns.

'You crazy critter!' he cussed, leaping into his saddle and spurring his reluctant horse into a gallop. 'You've ruined everythin' with yer foolin'!'

A ragged volley followed him, but he didn't fire back. His one idea now was to get back to the camp, and he saw no sense in wasting lead on such indifferent targets.

He didn't exert his mount too much; he knew that by the time the men had saddled up he would be far away, out of sound as well as sight. He didn't expect any serious pursuit, and in fact none came. But now they had been alarmed he knew it would be useless to try and surprise them again that night.

Rip rode out to challenge him. His voice sounded relieved when Tombstone called back. The big puncher said, 'What's the matter, kid? Scared?'

'Scared nuthin,' rapped the kid. ' 'Bout an hour ago I heerd a gun go off, back where that *hombre* had stood watching. You didn't come, an' I was sure you'd got hit an' been captured an' taken away.'

He didn't say that he'd called one of the men out to take his place, and then he'd gone forward and searched but found nothing.

Tombstone briefly told him what had happened, then went in and gave a fuller report to Mark Enty.

'Thar's about six of 'em,' he said. 'What they're up to, I cain't guess. But they're up to no good, as you said. Honest men don't go standing watching you from thorn thickets.' But what puzzles me is the way my hoss behaved. Until tonight it's always been a perfectly trained cowpony. But tonight—' He relapsed into helpless silence. He just couldn't understand it.

'Maybe yore stallion got wind of a mare,' said Enty.

Tombstone shook his head. 'That's no good as an explanation,' he said. 'My hoss's trained to stand still even with a dozen mares around. No, Mark, the puzzling thing to me is this – my hoss seemed to recognize those other hosses. Now, what does that mean, because I don't under-stand it myself?'

Mark said, 'It couldn't be a party you know, could it? Mebbe some more o' yore boys have drifted from that last ranch you were at. Mebbe the gold fever's got a few more on to the trail. That would account fer yore hoss gettin' excited, if it smelled some of its old stablemates around.'

Tombstone said, 'If they are some of the boys from the Maxie spread, you c'n bet they're not after gold.'

Enty looked at him sharply. 'Then what would they be after, on this trail?'

Tombstone grinned, rising. 'They'll be after stretching my neck on a rope,' he said, and then went out to relieve the kid.

Next morning the three punchers had a council of war. Tombstone said, 'It might be a party from Maxie, and mebbe Maxie's one of 'em, too. Don't fergit, Dutch Maxie's a mean, vindictive coyote – an' we've laid hands on him, quite apart from shootin' up a few of his boys. He's capable of trailing us for a week, in order ter git his revenge, the pizenous ol' rattlesnake.'

Corny said, 'Yeah, but he's not likely to attack us when we're with the wagons – we outnumber him, easily.'

'We sure do. But he might try an' pick us off when we're out-ridin'. So – today, pardners, ride closer in than usual. Keep yore eyes skinned, an' take no chances. *Sabe?*'

If he had only known, a few miles back down the trail a man was saying, 'They won't be carrying it with them. You bet it's hidden among them wagons. We gotta find a way of gittin' holt o' them prairie schooners. . . .'

If Tombstone had heard what the *hombre* was saying, he would have been more mystified than ever.

CHAPTER FOUR

WAR PAINT

Enty was striding around the camp, filling his lungs with sound and getting the wheels moving. This was the sixth morning since the three punchers had joined him outside Santa Fe. The previous afternoon, Corny had come streaking in, flat on the back of his horse, to report the presence of Indians in the neighbourhood.

'There were tracks, a mile south and a bit ahead of us,' he panted. 'I did some scouting and found they led to an Indian village 'way back o' that bluff thar. Thar's mebbe three or four dozen tepees, mebbe a few dozen braves.'

Enty said, 'They're probably harmless,' but that night he doubled the guard, all the same. And this morning he was in a hurry to move out of the district, because he didn't believe in inviting disaster. Five wagons was a very small train. . . .

They were travelling south of the more usual trail into Santa Fe, but that was because the pioneers' destination lay a few hundred miles south of Sacramento, where the gold strike was on. Even so, others used this trail, too, probably in an effort to miss the worst of the Mohave

Desert by traversing Death Valley and then skirting north-wards into the Californian hills beyond.

As they creaked and groaned their way up hill and down dale, they could see that just ahead of them was another wagon train. Tombstone kept examining the tracks and decided that it was a larger train than their own, probably amounting to at least a couple of dozen wagons. Even that was still a small train for such a long and hazardous undertaking, here in the rugged, hostile West.

About noon Rip came riding in to say that he'd spotted a party of horsemen away out on his flank. 'There was six. They weren't Injuns.'

'Mebbe they're our friend the watcher and his comrades,' said Tombstone. 'What were they up to?'

Rip waited until a girl on a pony got out of earshot, and then he said, 'They looked ter me ter be tryin' to git between me an' the wagons.'

'Tryin' ter cut you off, huh?' Tombstone was startled. He sat his horse and considered, then turned and went galloping through the choking dust along the line of wagons in search of the train boss. When he found him, he called him out to one side. They let the train go on. Rip joined them, but Corny was riding out in front.

Tombstone put the matter to Enty. 'We were grubstaked ter try an' keep danger away from you,' he said. 'Wal, it looks mighty like we're bringing danger to you. I'm seri-ously wondering if you'd be better off without us, Mark.'

Enty didn't like that, and he looked a very worried man. 'Trouble is, I need you boys. We've a long way ter go, an' God knows what danger lies around the corner. Sides.' he ended, 'ef you're in danger it's fer us ter try an' help you out of it, same's you do fer us.'

'The difference,' Tombstone pointed out, 'is that you've got wimmin an' kids ter look after.'

'All the same,' said Enty, 'I don't like the idea of you boys leavin'. I think you'd better stay on.' He looked very worried, and stood for a while watching back the way that Rip said he'd last seen the mysterious riders.

Tombstone rode for the next half hour in silence, not speaking to anyone. Then suddenly he spurred up to one of the wagons and asked Enty's son to relieve him while he rode forward. Corny saw him coming up and wondered. Tombstone didn't stay long with him.

He told of the men that Rip had seen, and then he said, 'I'm going ahead ter meet up with the other wagon train. I want to persuade 'em ter wait fer us to catch up with 'em. I'd feel happier if we had more company.'

Corny said, 'Mebbe Enty will keep us rollin' after dark, if that way we can catch up with the other party?'

Tombstone said, 'Not Enty. He won't take risks. He knows it's too dangerous, travelling when the light's gone. No, these other people must hold up for a few hours so as to let us join 'em. That is, if they're not too far ahead.'

Then he went riding off, his horse cantering at a smart pace that would soon leave the slow-moving schooners far behind. He didn't need to dismount to follow the tracks, because the recent passage of a couple of dozen heavy wagons wasn't hard to see, not on the dry, powdery soil of northern Arizona. It seemed to Tombstone that the tracks might be as recent as yesterday – which could mean that they were a couple of miles ahead or more than twenty!

A couple of hours passed. The sun was high now, and very hot. On all sides the hilly country was yellowing under the dry heat of the early summer. Tombstone sat his horse and sweated, and the rivulets coursed down the fine powder that settled on his face and seemingly left tear-stains.

As time went on, he grew anxious. If they were too far

ahead, it wasn't likely that they would stop and wait for them to catch up; making up ten or twelve miles was asking a lot from their own teams and couldn't be done in less than several days. Not here in this rough country, Tombstone thought, with the wheels biting deep into the encumbering dirt.

All at once he stopped. His keen eyes had caught a sign.

'Injuns!' he breathed, startled. An Indian trail led parallel to the wheel tracks. After a while, when the trail passed through bushes he saw more Injun sign, and he knew it to be a war party.

That made him more cautious, but it didn't turn him back. Just a little later he suddenly heard the crackle of rifle fire, and distant war whoops. He thought, 'The varmints, they're opening up an attack on the train.'

Now he spurred faster, though keeping well into the cover at the side of the trail. A few minutes later he came out at the head of a short cliff which gave an uninterrupted view across the bush-spattered plain beyond. He reined. There was no need to go further.

Less than half a mile away was the wagon train, circled up. Around it, screaming their terrifying war whoops, rode the attacking braves. Tombstone took a swift count and reckoned there must have been all of two hundred Indians in the attack, with possibly more held in reserve down one of the wooded arroyos, where the plumed chiefs sat their horses. The defenders were fighting like seasoned men – there was no frantic discharge of rifles in an effort to intimidate the naked braves; instead came the occasional crack of a carefully sighted weapon. Powder and shot were more precious than gold, here in the middle of the American Continent; it had be used carefully, to the best advantage.

As Tombstone watched, he saw the Indians, upon a

signal, turn their horses into a mad charge against the wagons. Then the ragged rifle fire of the defenders briskened into a sustained volley. The cowboy saw Indian after Indian go tumbling off his plunging pony, and felt that this was another attack that would be beaten off.

So it was. In the manner of Indian warfare, within seconds the attack was over, and the braves were streaming back out of distance of those deadly long rifles of the settlers. Back they went, to where their chiefs and medicine men stood awaiting them.

But they didn't go.

They held palava, and Tombstone knew what that meant. Now the braves would try other tactics, possibly flaming arrows, or perhaps they would set fire to the dry grass and try and burn the defenders out, or they might maintain seige until their water was finished. With such a large force the advantage was with the attackers.

Tombstone pulled his horse round cautiously and went galloping back along the trail. As he rode he hated himself for what he was doing – running away. But there was nothing else for it.

His duty was to warn Mark Enty that his few wagons were driving on to a large hostile party of Indians. Mark's best bet was to turn off the track and head due north for at least a day, before bearing west again.

What Tombstone would have to advise Enty was to run away and leave the other party to fight their own battles, and he didn't like the idea. But they had too few men to guard their own wagons, and none could be spared to go forward and try and assist the hard-pressed wagon train ahead.

Tombstone found himself wishing that he had just a few men. . . .

He saw horsemen right in his track, wheeling across it

to stop him. He saw a rope spinning in the air – it gripped his arms and he began a slow tumble out of his saddle. Then he hit the ground, and for a few seconds found himself being dragged.

And then the men were all round him, looking far away against the blue morning sky from where Tombstone lay among their horses' hoofs.

The men ... Jep Shaker, Edge Feodor, Kay Jimpsie ... Tombstone twisted and squinted against the light and saw Jup Farish, Nutty Din and Blat Wheddon. Just as tough a bunch of thugs as ever gave a fellar a rope collar without a trial.

And that, Tombstone felt, was close to their minds at that moment.

Jup Farish swung down and took his guns away. Then Jimpsie pulled on the rope and hauled him to his feet. Jep Shaker's eyes were slits of venomous hatred. He wasn't the kind to forgive a reverse such as he had experienced back in Santa Fe, and these days of stalking in this inhospitable near-desert land had tried his snapping temper to the utmost. Tombstone knew that he couldn't expect much in that direction.

Shaker said, 'You know why we bin follering yer, Tombstone?'

The big puncher didn't bother to reply.

Shaker motioned with his head. 'Fix his hands behind his back an' get him on his hoss. Thar's a tree over thar with a good high branch stickin' out. Reckon we c'n put it ter some purpose.'

Tombstone stared, while his hands were being tied. What was behind all this? Men didn't usually trail a man so far just for the pleasure of seeing him strung up, not at the behest of some aggrieved party, even though it was the boss.

He said, 'Dutch Maxie should ha' come along an' done his own dirty work.'

Shaker said, 'You smashed his fingers when you kicked his gun out of his hand. It ain't no good chasin' *hombres* like you ef you cain't tote a shooter. So we're kinda deputisin'.'

Tombstone said, 'I wish I'd ha' smashed his neck.'

'Might ha' bin better at that,' said Shaker nastily.

They'd got Tombstone on to his horse under the tree now, and Jimpsie was tossing the rope over. Feodor rode up and put the noose round the puncher's neck.

Shaker said, 'Ef you don't talk, you're a fool. There are three of you in the know, I reckon, an' if we dispose of you one of them kids c'n be made to open up.'

Tombstone said, 'I don't know what the hell you're talking about.' And then anger flooded into him as he remembered the urgency of things.

'While you're playin' at sher'fs, thar's a war party o' Injuns less'n two miles away, an' they've got a wagon train tied up. Thar's a coupla hundred o' the varmints. Ef you was men, you'd ride through an' give 'em a hand. Guess they could do with six more fightin' men.'

That stopped the men, for a moment. Tombstone saw they were listening. He strained his ears, but over the whole land there was a profound and peaceful silence. Evidently the Indians hadn't opened up a second attack.

Shaker broke the silence, roughly. 'He's stringin' us along. Thar ain't no Injuns this side o' the Colorado River. Pull on that rope; I ain't in the mood ter play long with this galoot. Reckon them kids might be easier ter open up an' we'll catch 'em.'

Tombstone felt the rope tighten, stretching his neck. It wasn't comfortable, sitting there at the end of a rope, with his hands tied behind his back.

Shaker said, 'Talk, pardner. Talk fast an' plenty if you want ter save yer neck.'

Jimpsie slackened off at a signal. Tombstone eased his neck and said, 'Talk about what?' Maybe it was the fall that had dazed him, but he didn't understand what Shaker was getting at.

Shaker snarled with fury, 'You know what. Quit stallin'. I ain't in the mood fer fun right now. Whar's it hidden? In them wagons?'

Tombstone sat there, not understanding. Where was what hidden? His silence goaded Shaker into a further paroxysm of rage.

'Ef yer play dumb, I'll see yer stay dumb, *hombre*. Ef you don't tell whar it's hidden, Jimpsie hyar'll pull on the rope until you're blue in the face. Ef yore neck don't break, I reckon you'll be talkin' fast, after five minutes o' that treatment.'

Tombstone said, tiredly, 'I guess this sun's too hot on yore head. I don't know what'n hell you're talkin' about.'

Shaker grinned wolfishly. 'Mebbe we c'n help that memory o' your'n. Up with him, Jimpsie.'

Tombstone felt the noose suddenly tighten. Then Edge Feodor spoke. He called, 'Hold on, Jep. Listen, thar's firin'!'

Shaker snarled, 'Ter hell with firin'! Get this galoot strung up!'

Feodor came shoving forward on his mount. 'You crazy fool,' he snarled. 'Ef these air Injuns, we got more important things ter do than stretchin' some varmint's neck fer the sake of Dutch Maxie.'

Shaker whirled in fury. 'You take orders from me, Feodor. He's goin' up. We're gonna get the truth outa him ef we've got to string him up for half a day.'

Feodor said, 'Let him down, Jimpsie.' That got the foreman clawing round in his saddle. Shaker wasn't a man to see authority slide into someone else's grasp.

But Feodor was holding a gun. He said, evenly, 'I don't want ter use this hyar pistol, Jep. Ef I do, that'll bring some o' the varmints after us, an' we don't stand much chance without rifles. So keep them hands clear o' yore holsters.'

Tombstone was watching the puncher, hope rising. And yet the turn of events was mystifying. Feodor was the last man he'd have thought of to start talking about doing something for hard-pressed settlers. He was a mean man to cross; a close, suspicious *hombre*, with rarely a good word for anything. Which, thought Tombstone, goes to show that you can't judge a man with accuracy even though you've shared the same bunkhouse for months with him. Feodor was rapidly taking charge.

'Cut Tombstone loose,' he ordered. 'Reckon we'll need his two guns soon. When we've finished this schemozzle, reckon we c'n start whar we left off. It's a big country, Tombstone, but you cain't get yerself lost from us in it. Now tell us about these Indians.'

Tombstone rubbed his wrists, then accepted the guns that Jup Farish rather doubtfully handed back on the order of Feodor. He said, 'I'll remember that, Feodor. The postponed necktie party. I mean.'

Then he told them about the strength and location of the attack and defence. 'They're strong, them settlers, shootin' like men. Mebbe they c'n hold out a long time yet; only thing is, I'm skeered o' some Injun trick they might think up.'

Feodor was taking it very calmly. He said, 'Thar's six o' us. That ain't many, though it's as good as thirty or forty redskins any day. Now, ef only we had another six, that'd be a sizeable party. These redskins soon git disheartened ef they think thar's reinforcements ridin' in.'

Tombstone sat his horse and did some thinking. He could see that while seven men – including himself – was quite a welcome addition to the beseiged force, it was probably insufficient to tip the scales in their favour. He thought about those five or six extra men that Feodor wanted, and wondered what Mark Enty would have to say about it.

The crackle of rifle fire rose to a sustained volley, then died away into an irregular crackle. 'Another attack beaten off,' thought Tombstone. 'Only it can't go on much longer like this.'

Feodor said, roughly, 'What're you thinkin', pardner? You'd better do yer thinking faster, 'cause I guess them settlers ain't in a very comfortable position right now.'

Tombstone said, 'Thar's eleven men back with my train. Mark Enty might take a risk an' hole up an' send half his force along to help out. That might be big enough to kid the Injuns that thar's help cumin' up in strength.'

Jep Shaker spurred across the path. 'You ain't goin' ter leave us, Tombstone. This is a trick ter git away from us. I ain't standin' fer it. He'll go an' we'll wait an' he'll never come back.'

Tombstone pulled round and faced the other men. He said, 'I'll come back. That's my word on it.'

'That's good enough fer me,' said Feodor, and Nutty Din and Wheddon nodded agreement, too. 'I reckon you're straight enough, apart from what you did ter Maxie, an' mebbe you got cause ter do that on the ol' rustler, anyway.'

Jep Shaker didn't like it, but he had to pull back and let Tombstone through. The big puncher said, 'If I go hell for leather, I c'n be back in just over an hour. I reckon all this time Enty's wagons'll have been gettin' nearer. I'll meet you back where the trail goes down the bluff. Ef the settlers is too hard-pressed, don't wait but go in.'

He sent his horse rearing round at that and then went hurtling back along the trail. He went fast, but not so fast as to blow his mount. There would be no spare horses back with Enty's train, so that his mount would have to bring him all the way back again.

He had a good horse, and it was in fine condition. The miles seemed to leap back as the long-striding beast settled down to a steady gallop.

So it was that far sooner than he had anticipated, Tombstone came upon the wagon train lumbering along up the track. Corny was well out in front. Tombstone didn't pause; as he came up he yelled, 'Fall back, Corny; I want you.'

Mark Enty was walking by the lead horses. Tombstone pulled up in a flurry of dust and pebbles, his hand raised to signal the train to stop. Two or three of the men came running up. Tombstone sent one of them galloping away to fetch in Rip and the other outriders.

He was panting, but he hadn't time to get his breath. 'Mark,' he said, 'thar's a big train, six or seven miles ahead, holed up by Injuns.'

'Injuns!'

The startled exclamation from Enty seemed to spread like flame through dry grass down the length of the wagon train. Tombstone saw the women turn into their wagons and then reappear with guns.

'Yeah, Injuns. Reckon thar's a coupla hundred at least. They're holdin' 'em off, but them Injuns is out fer blood.' Then he told, very briefly of his meeting with Jep Shaker and the T-over-X waddies.

'It kinda surprised me, Edge Feodor comin' up like that. Reckon thar's more sand ter the galoot than we thought, eh, Corny?'

'You're wantin' more men?' guessed Enty, and the old worry came back to his face.

'Reckon that's about it.' Tombstone nodded. 'Feodor's got some idea that if we just go hell-bent into them varmints when they're attackin' they'll git ter hell outa Arizona thinking thar's plenty reinforcements comin' up.'

'Could be,' said Enty. 'These Injuns is dogs – they'll scare easy, ef you run at 'em. But I don't like splitting up. Ef the Injuns get on our trail, what chance would we have?'

'I know,' said Tombstone. He wanted to help the beseiged settlers, but it was unfair to ask Enty to throw his own train into deadly peril. All Enty need do now was strike north out of danger.

But Enty wasn't that kind of man. He was an old-time pioneer, and these old-timers banded together in the face of their implacable, unrelenting enemy, the Red man. His instincts were all against deserting the settlers along the trail.

He spat tobacco juice thoughtfully, and watched the stain slowly soak into the fine dust as if it would reveal some message to him. Then he said, 'Reckon we c'n take a chance at that. Back a mile or so thar's a coulee. Reckon we could pull right in off the track an' brush away our trail so's even an Injun wouldn't know we'd holed in thar. Reckon we'd be safe fer today, anyway, with only a few men ter handle the wagons.'

'That means you'll lend some men?'

'Sure. We cain't leave them settlers to be tomahawked by them red varmints, can we?' There was a murmur of approval from the other settlers. They left Enty to make the decisions, but it was plain that this was a popular one with them, even though it cast danger upon their own families and possessions.

'Reckon I'll keep one man ter each wagon, only,' said Mark. 'That's five. Some o' the ten-year-olds c'n use a gun pretty good, an' with them an' the women, mebbe we'll manage.'

That gave Tombstone another five men, including Rip and Corny. The five went racing off to get their horses, while the men who were to remain behind whipped the wagons into a turn and began to head back down the trail again.

Tombstone, Rip, Corny and another man set off at a canter. After a few minutes the other two men came riding up. Tombstone saw that one was Enty's son. He was a bit young, but a good fighter.

Half an hour later they came flogging their horses up to the edge of the cliff. As they rode they could hear steady firing, and guessed that another attack was developing. Tombstone saw the T-over-X men back of some trees that leaned as if a wind had blown them over – as indeed it had. But it gave good cover from the Redskins.

Feodor said, 'Good. I knew you'd come back, Tombstone. And a dozen of us – that's good!'

Tombstone said, 'What's in yore mind, Feodor?'

'We're gonna wait until a big attack develops. Then we'll ride among 'em, yellin' our heads off, an' doin' as much damage as we can. Ef them settlers is seasoned fighters they'll know to come out shootin' when they see us. That way them Injuns won't know how many of us have just arrove.'

'You've done this before?'

'Once't. But it was north, against the Sioux tribes before they were driven from Ohio. We hit 'em so hard an' sudden plumb in the middle o' their attack, that they shut their mouths and streaked like lightning to their squaws and papooses. They didn't stop to see how many of us there was; they jes' nacherly assumed we must be an over-whelming force, otherwise we wouldn't dare attack. Mebbe we c'n surprise these Injuns jes' the same way today.'

They stood and waited. At the moment the Indians were attacking by stealth, crawling under cover and trying to pick off the defenders with old guns and bows and arrows. But back down the wooded arroyo they could see the main force assembling again for another attack.

Wheddon was saying. 'They'll be tryin' flamin' arrows soon; they always do. You watch them skulking varmints; they're crawling near fer jes' that reason.'

But Tombstone wasn't watching. Away north, across a dried creek bed, he had seen a movement. He called, 'Out of sight, everyone! Thar's Injuns comin'!'

They pulled deeper into the brush, while Tombstone and Corny went forward on their faces so as to watch the approaching enemy. In a few moments they saw the party – there were six or seven naked braves, faces hideous with white streaks that splayed out from their noses to their ears.

Tombstone whispered, 'Corny, they got someone! Thar's someone slung across in front o' one o' them Injuns. Mebbe it's one o' the settlers, caught out huntin'.'

Nearer came the little war party. Then they heard sounds from the plain, and Rip came scrambling up to say that the Injuns were setting up another attack. 'Thar ain't much firin' from the wagons now,' said Rip, as an after-thought. 'Mebbe they're runnin' outa powder an' shot.'

'Or outa men,' said Tombstone, and then he gripped Corny so hard that his fingers bruised. 'Look at that!' His voice startled the boy. He looked.

'Hully gee,' he exclaimed. 'A gal!'

They could see her long yellow hair against the dark of

53

the Indian pony, as she lay inert across its back, the brave sitting behind her.

Back on the plain the firing now rose to a crescendo. The attack was in full swing. The little war party below quickened its pace, as if anxious to get into the fighting. From behind they heard Feodor's impatient voice, 'What's holdin' yer, Tombstone? Now's our chance!'

Tombstone went back like a great crab, keeping under cover the whole way. 'Right,' he said. 'Let's get out. Only let me get ahead of you. Thar's an Injun with a white gal, an' I aim ter settle fer him afore anyone knows we're comin'.'

With that he spurred his horse away, down to the soft sand of the dried creek. He took a risk on making a noise, though it wasn't a great one because the sand cushioned most sounds, and when he came round the corner after the Indians he was going full tilt.

They didn't suspect that anything was amiss as his horse came nosing into the party; their thoughts were too intent on the battle still out of sight from them.

Tombstone didn't want to use his gun until the last moment. He swung up against the brave who was carrying the girl in front of him . . . saw the brave turning suddenly towards him . . . saw sharp brown eyes, broad cheekbones . . . a mouth opening to shout.

But even as the brave was turning, Tombstone was striking him off his horse. It was a quick swing with his left hand – rigid, it crashed into the brave's neck, for a second paralysing him. He started to go down; then, to his horror, Tombstone saw the girl slipping off the horse.

The other braves were turning . . . and Tombstone knew that he hadn't time to stop and pick her up.

CHAPTER FIVE

JEP SHAKER
GETS CONTROL

Tombstone went for his guns, lips curling in a snarl. But there were five braves, and they were coming in fighting. He saw the white war paint, the mouths opening in screaming, terrifying war whoops. Saw the tomahawks and rifles in their hands and started firing.

But he wouldn't move from over the girl. He'd come to rescue her, and he would go down fighting rather than run away. His guns started coming up. But the braves weren't more than five yards away, coming in fast. . . .

Someone yelled, 'Git goin' ' and something slapped his horse and sent it plunging madly sideways. That gave Tombstone some room. His guns took the first brave right off his raw-hide-blanket saddle. They blatted flame again and he saw that he had hit a second brave, though he didn't come out of his saddle. It was difficult, hitting swift-moving targets from the back of a prancing horse.

All the same, his mount was moving round with effect. That sideways plunge had put them on the flank of the remaining four Indians and they were pulling round but getting in each other's way.

Tombstone realized that someone was holding on to his stirrup.

He hit a brave full in the chest as he came at him, then shot the horse from under another. Rip, flying up, opened on the remaining mounted Indian, missed, but it put the brave to flight in terror.

He went careering round on to the plain, convinced that an army was hurtling down after him.

Tombstone looked down. The girl was clinging to his stirrup. She was wearing buckskin shirt and trousers and could have passed for a boy but for her long, corn-yellow hair. He saw blue eyes; then lips opened in a smile at him.

'Nice work, cowboy,' she called. 'Gimme a hand up.'

Tombstone holstered his guns, swung down and hoisted the girl up behind him, just as the rest of the party came thundering up. They went streaking round that bend as if all the furies in hell were after them.

'Noise!' yelled Feodor, and they knew what that meant.

The braves, riding in from a contracting circle, hadn't expected this. One minute they were doing all the attacking; the next a screaming horde of palefaces seem to have sprung from nowhere, their deadly, close-range six-shooters doing incredible damage. They seemed to be everywhere, these new attackers, riding in amongst the startled, milling braves, now no longer shrilling their war whoops.

Panic rose in their savage hearts. The thunder of the six-shooters dinned at point-blank range in their ears, and Indian after Indian went crashing down, to lie twitching on the sun-warm earth. At that range they couldn't miss; every shot found a target – and killed.

Just as their six-guns were emptying, the settlers came sallying out on foot, cheering madly. It provided the diversion required to give the cowboys time to load up again.

The settlers came running out, knelt, aimed and fired. Then they were out still farther, knelt again, aimed – and another volley swept more Indians on to the ground.

The punchers had reloaded. They went smoking into those Indians, roaring their heads off, guns blazing and bringing death to the naked red men.

Panic took charge then. One or two faint hearts turned and bolted; in a moment quite a bunch had separated and were galloping off. Fresh bodies of Indians, riding up, saw them scurrying away – they didn't ask questions; they assumed the worst and joined in the headlong retreat.

Feodor screamed. 'Keep 'em going! Harry 'em as long as you can.' And he went plunging after the redskins, his gun blatting fire as fast as he could turn it on to a target.

They chased the redskins for about a mile, then decided that it wasn't wise to go further. Tombstone had dropped the girl and was with them, and he it was who ordered them all back. There was no sense in losing their advantage by riding into an Injun trap. So back they came, slowly this time, on to the battlefield.

The carnage looked terrible. A few Indians were crawling painfully away. They let them go. A wounded Indian was a good advertisement to the power of the white man to hurt. Looking around, Tombstone reckoned that in that latest mêlée, something like sixty redskins had been either killed or wounded.

But the Paleface hadn't got off scot free. During the battle losses had been accepted with no more than a tightening of the lip and a greater determination to shoot down the savage redskins. But once the battle was over, reaction set in.

Trotting towards the line of wagons, Tombstone could hear the sound of women weeping for the men who had started off but would never get nearer to California than this blood-soaked square of Arizona soil. And children were wailing. . . .

One of the settlers caught hold of Tombstone's stirrup on the way back. He told the big puncher that they had lost at least a dozen people killed, and many more had received injuries.

'It's hit us hard,' he said. He was a fair-haired boy with a northern accent. 'We ain't got many men now ter see us through. A couple o' kids an' three or four women stopped lead in that shindy, too.'

There was great activity around the camp lines. Men were hurrying off to get water, in case the seige was laid again; other parties were going out to bury the dead, redman as well as paleface. The wounded were receiving attention from the women, while other women cooked a meal over the several fires that had been started. Even the children were helping.

Everywhere was this bustle of concentrated effort. Time was precious; the train boss wanted to get through this hostile country before another attack could be launched.

Tombstone came riding in. Suddenly he reined. A man lay stretched before him, his skull split open to a tomahawk blow. Tombstone said to himself, 'You was goin' ter stretch my neck, pardner, but I still cain't help feelin' sorry fer the way you've passed out.'

Then he rode on, and that was his epitaph for Kay Jimpsie, the man with an all-powerful hurry to use a rope.

Nearer camp still he saw Rip and another of Enty's men gently carrying in a sagging figure.

'Who's that?' Tombstone asked, and his mind framed the word, 'Corny?' But it wasn't; it was young Enty, in a bad way.

Rip said, 'He's gotta be good, ter pull outa this one.

Reckon I'd better go fer his father, pronto.'

'Don't start alone,' Tombstone ordered. 'That trail might be watched. When we go back, we're goin' in force.'

An oldish black-eyebrowed man detached himself from the throng where the wounded were receiving treatment. He walked up with his hand outstretched. 'You're Tombstone?' The puncher nodded. 'They tell me we're indebted ter you fer this timely rescue, pardner.'

'No more'n a dozen other *hombres*,' said the cowboy, bending to shake hands. 'But we ain't got time ter talk. Did my boys tell yer that we're with a train of five wagons, back aways down the trail?'

The wagon boss nodded.

'OK. Wal, they're purty near defenceless, an' I guess the next thing is ter take a strong party an' get 'em in afore them Injuns change their minds about running away.'

'You think they'll attack again?'

'I ain't no Injun scout, so I wouldn't know. Mebbe Enty's opeenion would be more vali'ble. All I know is, thar's still plenty redskins back in them hills, an' I don't believe in taking risks.'

'Right,' said the boss with decision. 'We'll call all the men in. How many do you require to bring the wagons up?'

Tombstone said, 'I don't know how many men of my own I can count on, now – I've seen a couple outa action, an' mebbe thar's more got hurt. Mebbe I've only got seven or eight all told, and we've only five men back with the wagons.'

The boss was watching the low hills where the plain ended. He said, 'I don't like it, but your boss risked his wagons to help us, an' I must risk mine ter bring him an' his people safely in. You're mighty vulnerable on that trail. Reckon I'd better let you have a dozen or fifteen men ter guard you. Ef we're attacked meanwhile, we'll jes' have ter wait until you come back ter help us.'

Tombstone nodded. 'Ef we're attacked, we'll abandon the wagons an' bring the people in behind us. That is, unless we have a chance to bring the train in safely. But I don't aim ter take no risks, and neither will Enty, I know.'

The train boss shouted to the men to come near. He himself had no idea what losses they had suffered during the fight, and his face fell as he saw the number of men who limped as they walked in, or who nursed broken limbs.

'Reckon a dozen's as much as I c'n spare,' he said to Tombstone. 'That leaves me with no more'n a dozen unwounded myself.'

'It'll have ter do.' Tombstone nodded agreement. His eyes were searching for members of his own party. Rip he'd seen, and a couple of the other settlers. Then he spotted Blatt Wheddon, with a bandage round his fore-arm, but he looked capable of riding and fighting . . . Jup Farish and Nutty Din didn't seem to be harmed . . . Jep Shaker, surly but unhurt . . . Edge Feodor with a bandaged shoulder.

'Hey, Edge, c'n you ride . . . an' fight?' he called.

Edge moved his shoulder doubtfully. 'Yeah, I reckon so,' he said at length, but Tombstone decided that Feodor wasn't to be regarded as a first-class fighting man.

Then Tombstone breathed a sigh of relief as Corny came galloping up ahead of the water party that he had been guarding. 'One man missing,' thought Tombstone, looking for the last settler from his party. He went down among the wounded and found him. His ankle was shat-tered, but he was smoking a corn cob stoically and didn't seem much worried. 'Jes' tell my wife I ain't more'n scratched,' he said. 'An' fetch my baccy, Tombstone; I'm goin' ter smoke a lot, these next days.'

That gave Tombstone ten men, and with the dozen that the wagon boss was lending them, they made up a formidable little party.

They waited long enough to grab something to eat and get a drink of scalding, reviving coffee, though the wait was more for the benefit of their hard-worked horses than for themselves. While Tombstone was drinking, he saw the girl that he had rescued start to walk towards him. He walked forward, removing his hat. She still wore shirt and pants of fringed buckskin, but now she'd tied her corn-bright hair back with a ribbon. She was a strong-looking, pleasant faced girl, lacking in gaucherie and shyness as indeed were most of these girls of the plains and the frontiers.

She held out her hand, and that set Tombstone a problem. He had hot coffee in one hand and a hat in the other. 'Reckon I could do with a third hand, right now,' he grinned.

She took his hand – the one holding his hat – in both of hers, laughing. 'You got enough fer me to hold on to, mister,' she smiled. 'That was timely of you, pickin' me up outa them Injuns. I'd sure given myself up for a goner. When you knocked that Injun off his hoss, I was so surprised I fell off myself.',

'That nearly spoiled things,' smiled Tombstone. 'Good job you weren't unconscious, as I thought was the case. How d'you come ter be with them varmints, anyway?'

The girl shrugged casually. 'We saw the Injuns soon after some men set off ter fill some water bar'ls at a spring we found way back o' them elms. Someone had ter ride an' fetch 'em in. I went, but the Injuns attacked afore we could get back. We laid low, but during the fighting a party o' braves came ridin' out ter git water. They musta seen our tracks an' they dug us out. We killed a couple, but our three boys got killed an' scalped. They spared me because I was a woman.'

'They wouldn't have spared you much, once they got you back to their camp,' said Tombstone grimly. 'Them squaws don't like paleface wimmin.'

The train boss called to him just them, so Tombstone said, 'Time ter go. Hope we'll be jinin' up with you soon. Good-bye, gal.'

'Goodbye, cowboy,' she called. 'An' good luck.'

Then she called him back, 'What's your name, cowboy?'

He grinned. 'Tombstone,' he said.

'Tombstone?' She looked at him, then said, 'That ain't a name, it's a destination.'

The puncher laughed and waved his hand and then rode away. The settlers turned out to watch them go. They knew that this was a dangerous mission, sending out part of their depleted strength in order to bring in five slow-moving wagons. There'd be plenty of scouting Injuns to see them on the march in.

There was no cheering as they trotted away, just a few hands waved in farewell. Tombstone looked round. The girl with the corn yellow hair saw his head turn and waved to him. Tombstone waved back.

Rip looked at Corny. 'My,' he said, 'this galoot sure knows how ter bring the shine to a gal's eyes.'

'Sure do,' said Tombstone evenly. 'You jes' take 'em off an Injun's hoss, that's all. You find yourself a gal like that, an' see how their eyes shine when you bring 'em home.'

Corny said, 'Me, I could fall fer a gal like that. Reckon ef we fix up together I'm a-goin' sparkin' that yaller-haired wench.'

'Yeah?' said Rip. 'Reckon I'll be sparkin' her myself. I always did like 'em with long yaller hair over their shoulders.'

Tombstone said, 'Don't mind me, pardners. I only found the gal.'

As they left the plain they fell into silence. There was too much cover close to the trail, and Tombstone didn't like it. If mounted Injuns chose to attack them anywhere along this track, they wouldn't stand much chance. A couple of miles down the trail it was especially bad. Tombstone drew rein at this point.

Low hills came to a point that narrowed the trail to no more than twenty or thirty yards in width. Tombstone said, 'Ef we get back hyar an' find a coupla dozen braves hid up on each side o' the trail, we'll never git through.'

He turned in his saddle. 'Reckon half a dozen o' you had better hole up on the high ground at each side o' the trail. You fellars with rifles are best. Keep outa sight until you have to fire. Ef we come a-runnin', hold any Injuns back as long as you can afore riding in behind us.'

They galloped on, leaving six men to hide their horses and then go to ground with their deadly long guns. Tombstone said, 'I feel better, knowin' we got that pass under our control. An' if we get through, they could hold up them blamed redskins mebbe long enough fer us ter make camp.'

Tombstone was thinking ahead.

So well had Enty covered his trail that they would have ridden past where their wagons were holed up, if the lookout man hadn't stood up and waved to them. Tombstone sent his horse kicking round in the dust and headed into the coulee.

Enty came forward, his face shining with relief and delight. The other settlers were beaming. Tombstone smiled, 'I'll bet it's bin harder fer you, waitin' an' wonderin' what's happened, than it has bin fer us.' Then he remembered the two injured men. 'Yore son's bin hurt,

Mark. Don't know how bad, but he's unconscious. Reckon you'd better ride on an' see him.'

Tombstone saw the blood start to drain out of Enty's face, then the train boss shook his head. 'My duty's with these wagons,' he said, and walked away. Tombstone rode forward and gave the news to the settler's wife. She merely nodded. Tombstone thought, 'She was so sure he'd never come back, a busted ankle don't seem alarming at all to her. Reckon she'll jes' make a big fuss of him when they meet up,'

The wagons were man-handled round in order to save time; the horses swiftly hitched on and whipped into motion. Everyone felt that it was a race against time. The moment their little train was spotted on the move, the war parties would gather until they had strength enough to ride down upon them and wipe them out.

Speed, speed! Seconds counted! Men and women worked with feverish haste to get the wheels a-rolling. Then they were all out across the rough land and on to the rutty trail beyond. Mark Enty looked down the line to see that every wagon was now ready to move. His hand began to raise, to give the signal to move, and then a thin, harsh voice stopped him.

'We helped you enough, Enty!' It was Jep Shaker speaking. 'We ain't going back into Injun country. We've come far enough as it is, an' I reckon this hyar's whar we split forces. We came fer Tombstone an' these kids, an' I reckon we'll be takin' 'em away from you.'

Tombstone looked. So did everyone else – the men, the women and their children. Even Farish, Wheddon, Feodor and Nutty Din seemed surprised at the unexpectedness of the interruption. Then Wheddon said, 'Yeah, I reckon Jep's right at that. We done enough Injun fightin' as it is.'

Tombstone's temper broke. 'Shaker, you goddam fool,

put yore gun up! We ain't got time fer arguments. Let's get these people into safety an' then we c'n talk.'

'I ain't foolin'.' Shaker's voice rasped jarringly to their ears. 'I didn't ask ter take part in no Injun warfare, an' I've had enough. We're goin', an' you're comin' with us.'

Jep Shaker didn't give a hang if the settlers were inconvenienced, if they were wiped out. There was only one person important in Jep Shaker's life. His name was Jep Shaker.

'Move, blast yer,' said Shaker quickly, his eyes darting from one man to another for the first sign of danger. 'You kids, too. Ef you don't move pronto I'll blow the brains outa the youngest kid!'

'Go on, do it,' said Rip truculently, but Tombstone told him to shut up and started to ride forward.

Then there was a curious interruption. One of the women came stepping resolutely forward. She was middle-aged, solid and strong, the mother of one of the boys in the party. She was a typical pioneering woman, with no frills and nonsense about her. In her hand was a long gun.

She came quietly forward and took hold of Shaker's horse by the bridle before he knew what she was up to. Then just as quietly she said, 'I don't know what you want these boys for, but we need 'em more'n you do. Besides, they're good boys, an' we owe 'em a lot. You ain't takin' them away, mister, not while I'm standin'.'

'We'll see about that,' began Shaker with a snarl, but you could see that he was uncertain, suddenly. You could shoot at a man, but no matter the circumstance, you daren't raise a weapon to a woman. Shaker knew that if he shot this woman, even his own men would turn against him. It was the code of the West, the code that good and bad obeyed. . . .

He spurred his horse, hoping to free its head, but the

woman held on and said, 'What're you gonna do for a horse, mister?' And he saw that her gun was digging into the throat of his mount.

Sweat broke out instantly on his forehead, and he gave in. Without a horse in this country, and with these settlers dead against him, he knew that he was a lost man.

The woman went on, never raising her voice, 'Jes' you put up yore guns an' ride away – all of you. Reckon we'll do better without men o' yore kind.'

Slowly Shaker obeyed, his face white with anger at being frustrated so simply by this solid, unprepossessing woman. But he obeyed. The guns went slowly into their holsters. Instantly Tombstone's guns leapt into his hands.

'That's good advice, Shaker. Git movin'. Thanks fer the help up ter now – but we'll manage without you, I reckon from now on.'

Jep Shaker raked his mare and sent it crashing back down the trail. The other four men rode off in a bunch just behind him. Enty said, 'It's a pity, though. We might need them guns o' their'n.' Then he gave the signal and the wagons lurched into movement.

Tombstone rode up to the last swaying wagon. The woman who had saved him was hauling on the long reins so as to free her man for fighting if it became necessary. He shouted above the cracking of whips and creaking of wheels, 'Thanks, maw. I sure owe you somep'n for that piece o' quick thinkin' on your part.'

She called down from her high seat, 'Au, think nothin' of it, cowboy. Jes' keep an eye on that boy o' mine, will yer?'

'I sure will, maw,' he promised, and then he went back to ride guard on the flank of the train.

He had placed the men far out from the trail, riding in a huge circle around the moving wagons. If they saw

Indians, they had to close in slowly, fighting for time all the way. Tombstone calculated that they had eight or nine miles to travel, which could take anything from an hour and a half to more than two hours.

At the moment they were pushing the straining wagon horses, though they weren't flogging them as they might have to do before the end of the journey. For the moment they seemed to be making nice going, but farther up the trail there were some bad spots which would slow them.

Only a few minutes after they had started to move, Tombstone heard the sound of shots behind them. First one, then about three in quick succession. Then silence. He looked at Corny, who was riding with him.

'Now, what does that mean?' he asked.

'It's come from the way Shaker an' his *hombres* have jes' gone,' said, Corny. 'Mebbe they've piled into a huntin' party already.'

'Anyway, them shots'll sure be heard by some Injun who'll come investigatin'. Reckon it's done the damage, so far as we're concerned.'

He rode forward and told Enty, who hadn't heard because of the noise from the straining, creaking wagons. 'Git 'em movin' a bit faster, Mark,' he advised. 'I got six men holed up 'bout five miles along the trail. Ef we start a fight with Injuns I'd like 'em ter be near enough ter jine us.'

Mark Enty nodded and spurred forward again and whipped the leading horses into greater activity. Tombstone dropped well to the rear, along with the two kids. He wanted to spot danger at the earliest possible moment, and he felt that it would probably come from the direction of those shots.

Hardly was he back in position when Rip reined in, saying, quickly, 'Listen, hosses!'

They listened. There was the drum of horses' hoofs, hard-pressed along the trail behind them. The three drew their guns and turned to face the oncoming riders. Suddenly they came into view around a screen of thorns.

Rip said, 'Feoder!' astonished.

Feodor and Jup Farish came galloping up. Feodor was grinning, though his face looked pale from the loss of blood he'd suffered with his shoulder wound.

'We changed our minds,' grinned Feodor. 'We thought we'd like ter try our hands at gold-minin' in Californy, so we came back.'

Tombstone looked at him for a second. He wasn't kidded. If Feoder had wanted to go, the short way to the strike, the safest way, he'd have done better to have struck north until he reached the main, busy trail. Feodor had come back because he knew that the settlers needed every pair of guns they could get – and the hands to trigger them.

He nodded. 'I'll remember this, Feodor,' he said. 'An' you, too, Jup.' These men seemed only bad when they had someone like Dutch Maxie and Jep Shaker to shove them into brutality. . . .

'What about that shooting?' he asked.

Feodor and Farish exchanged glances. Feodor said, 'When I told Shaker I wasn't goin' along with him, he went fer his gun. I reckon he'd bin shoved around too much today an' he'd had enough of it. Wal, I knew he'd do that, so I was a split second faster on the draw. I got him first shot. He fell outa his saddle pullin' on the trigger but he only skeered a lark, I reckon.'

Tombstone looked at him. 'Shaker?'

'Yeah, he won't shake no more,' said Feodor laconically.

'What about Wheddon an' Nutty Din?'

'They jes' sat their hosses, not makin' ter interfere.

68

Reckon they felt it was none o' their business. Jup didn't jine in, either. When it was over we had a talk, and then Jup said he'd come with me but the others said they'd had enough of Injun country an' were goin' back ter Santa Fe. I wanted ter bring Shaker's hoss along as a spare, but they wanted it, too, so we tossed up fer it and I lost.'

Tombstone grinned at the slow, dry explanation. 'Reckon you'd better shove up an' tell Mark Enty you're here. He'll be mighty glad ter have you.'

Rip called, 'An' keep yore eyes skinned fer Injuns. Them shots'll sure bring 'em outa their crutches, I guess.'

They watched the two punchers go riding swiftly into the dust that was churned waist high along the track. They saw them politely touch their hats to the woman driving the rear team, and then go up to where Enty was helping a labouring team to negotiate some soft earth spots that gave no grip to the iron-rimmed wheels.

'Bet she got a surprise, seein' 'em so soon,' Corny grinned, and then the two punchers came riding back to join Tombstone and his buddies.

Time passed. The sun was on its last quarter. The horses were weary now, yet they had more than half their journey still to accomplish. But hope was rising within the settlers' breasts.

'Mebbe the varmints missed them shots,' said Corny, at length. 'Give us another quarter of an hour on the road and we'll be up to where our other men are holed up.'

The tension began to decrease all the way up the line. You could feel the change, riding along. People were smiling again, nodding to you, and the grim lines had smoothed away. They weren't out of danger yet, by a long way, but by heaven they'd come farther than they'd ever expected to get!

So they went on. Sometimes a wagon would stick, and

then horsemen would come crashing in, hurtling off their mounts and straining at the wheels. Once the wagon was moving, they'd climb back to their saddles and space out on the flank again, alert and watchful.

Another half mile . . . another mile. Then Enty waved back to them. 'Now, what does that mean?' Feodor asked.

'He c'n probably see the hills where our other men are laying up. Guess they can't be more'n a mile or so ahead, then.'

'Nearly home,' Corny was saying, breathing a deep sigh of relief. 'Nearly home. . . .'

Then Tombstone was standing erect in his stirrups, his face taut, his eyes straining. A rider far out on the southern flank was tearing in as fast as his pony could bring him.

'We're not home yet,' Tombstone said, touching spurs to his horse. 'My guess is that that *hombre*'s seen Injuns!'

CHAPTER SIX

RACE AGAINST DEATH

Over his shoulder he called, 'Stay where you are – except Corny. You come with me!'

They rode out to intercept the rider, who swerved towards them when he recognized the tall puncher. It was one of the men from the other wagon train.

'Injuns,' he shouted, reining. 'Thar's seven o' the varmints keepin' pace with us!'

'Sure thar ain't more?'

The man shrugged. 'Cain't be sartin, but them's all we've seen.

Tombstone said, 'Git back and keep watch on 'em.' Then he turned to Corny. 'Get Enty – tell him to go all out to reach them hills whar those other boys are hid up. Ef we git cut off afore we git thar, we'll all lose our scalps. Then go round the circle – tell the men thar's Injuns. Tell 'em to watch out and close in on the wagons ef they see me wavin' my hat. Tell 'em not ter come across ter me, even if thar's fightin', unless I send fer 'em. We gotta keep watch all the time, right round them wagons, an' not jest on one side.'

Corny spurred away, and Tombstone went galloping across to where a little bunch of men were keeping watch on the Indians.

Tombstone could see them quite plainly now. Because they knew they had been spotted, the Indians made no attempt to keep under cover. Tombstone counted, watching those nearly-naked men riding steadily abreast of them.

'Fifteen,' he said. 'They're getting reinforcements.'

One of the men said, 'Them varmints is in range now,' and started to level his gun. Tombstone stopped him.

'Don't waste shot. And don't send 'em under cover – it's better fer us ter see how quickly they are growing in number.'

They seemed to be getting reinforcements very quickly. In two or three minutes as many as thirty were boldly cantering parallel with them. And now they were getting bolder and were riding much closer in.

One of the men pointed. He didn't need to speak. Everyone looked. Back of the Indians a bush-choked gully emptied out into this valley through which they were so slowly moving. Every now and then they saw the feathered head-dress of mounted Indians momentarily in the gaps between the thorns.

'Thar's a big war party coming down that hill,' said Tombstone. 'Must be twenty or thirty in it. I reckon when they arrive the varmints'll feel strong enough to start an attack.'

He looked round. They were still a long way from that narrow pass. There was still time for the Indians to encircle them and cut them off from it. If they did . . .

Then the leading wagon got stuck, and the train came to a stop. Frantically men hurled their weight against the wheel and slowly started it to move again. Then the second wagon stuck in the same place . . . and the third.

They lost time badly then, just when they could least afford it. They were only just moving again when the big Indian war party streamed out and joined their fellows.

Tombstone sent Corny galloping back to pick up a few more men to guard this flank. Feodor and Farish came along leaving Rip alone in the rear. Then two other men rode up, both with long guns.

They had eight men here, facing a war party now grown to about fifty, with more Indians riding in every minute.

Tombstone said, 'Here it comes!' as the Indians ranged themselves out in a deep crescent. He shouted, 'They're goin' ter come ridin' in. Don't let 'em get in among you. Hold 'em back as much as you can, but fall back on to the wagons. We're not far from the gap, an' we might make it, though even then we're a long way from home.'

Enty had the wagons rolling smartly again, and the whips were cracking and the men were shouting and driving the horses as they had never been driven before. The terrified beasts plunged in their harness and dragged the weighty, covered wagons along at a speed dangerous on that rough ground. . . .

A wild scream and then the Indians came riding in, their war whoops shrilling across to where the little knot of palefaces awaited them. Tombstone saw that there was no stopping them, so he waved his hat in the air as a signal for all the outriders to close in on the wagons. That would give them greater strength when the attack came to close quarters.

The men with rifles opened fire and sent panic into the ponies by shooting several down. Then the Indians were coming into range of the small arms, and the battle really began.

The white men went back, but they didn't bolt. Every yard that they yielded, it cost an Indian his life. Back they went, and Indian after Indian came crashing from their half-wild ponies.

It still didn't stop them, but it kept them galloping out a bit, trying to get around the resolute little band of defenders. Then the fighting came close enough to the lumbering wagons for the other defenders to open up with their rifles. That made the Indians pull their horses' heads around and gallop quickly out of range. They had no weapons to match these fine long guns of the pioneers, which could kill at great distances.

Tombstone saw the danger first, because he was watching for it. The Indians were streaking ahead of the wagon train, trying to cut in front and stop it. If once they could stop the wagons, they knew that they could wipe out this tiny band of settlers.

Tombstone yelled, 'Follow me,' and settled down to foil the manoeuvre. He and half a dozen men shot ahead of the straining teams and raced forward to cut across the circling tracks of the Indians. They were only partly successful. The Indians, because of their superior weight of numbers, gradually forced their way towards the track along which the wagon train was moving.

Tombstone felt like groaning with despair. So near. . . .

The leading Indian somersaulted off his horse. The next horse went down. Then another Indian came sliding off. . . .

Tombstone thought, 'Someone's a mighty fine shot to do that from off the back o' a hoss.' And then he realized that none of his men was firing, that the shots hadn't come from his party.

Glad relief came over him. They must now be within range of the riflemen up by the pass. And because the

74

riflemen were prone on steady ground, they could inflict great losses upon the mounted Indians.

Another couple of Indians came crashing off. The warriors faltered, not understanding what was hitting them. Another horse went screaming on to its knees.

Tombstone roared, 'Attack – drive 'em off!'

If only they could drive the Indians back for as little as two minutes, that would permit the wagons to come within the protective fire of the hidden riflemen!

The Indians were shaken by that hidden rifle fire, so devastatingly accurate. When they saw Tombstone and his six comrades come tearing towards them they felt sure they had run into a trap, that there was a strong force of riflemen lying in wait to destroy them to a man. They had had experience of the white man's cunning in battle, and were ever afraid of being led into deadly ambushes.

They pulled away, not far, but sufficient to give the wagons passage. The heavy, swaying vehicles crashed towards the pass . . . entered it . . . and were through.

But they still had two miles to go, and their horses were in difficulties. Tombstone sent his panting horse up the sharp hillside to where the riflemen were lying. From the top he looked back.

The broadening valley behind seemed choked with Indians – now there must have been fifty of them, with small bands racing up in the distance, every minute adding to their number.

While he was watching, some of the Indians tried to charge the gap, but the long guns picked a couple off and at once the others wheeled away.

Tombstone shouted to six of the men to ride with the wagons. 'The rest o' you, string out atop the bluff,' he called. 'Hold 'em back as long as you can.'

That was still the tactic – delay the enemy as much as

posible . . . even seconds added up.

He saw the men fan out along the low ridge through which the track ran, dismounting when they were in position and running forward so as to command an open view across the way they had come.

The Indians were now streaming left and right of the trail, trying to spot an easy place which they could rush. But the hills grew higher and more precipitous, the farther they rode from the track.

After a time, screaming their war whoops, they streamed back, and then upon a signal they came hurtling in arrow formation on both sides of the track simultaneously. On the north side they were turned by the rapid, accurate fire from the defenders, but the war party on the south side found the way easier and came up with a rush. Even so, only a few got through, and they were driven off before a second attack was started.

There was a lull as the Indians galloped away out of range and held palava. The spirits of the defenders rose. The wagons were out of sight already. If only they could hold these varmints for another ten short minutes. . . .

A few minutes later they saw the second attack coming. As soon as it started, Tombstone knew that there was no holding it. The body of Indians came rolling across the level ground like some fleshy, irresistible juggernaut. Tombstone, on the north side, saw that they were heading for the weak place on the south bluff. . . .

He shouted, before the din of the whooping Indians could drown his voice, 'Do all the damage you can, but don't stay so long that you get cut off!'

Then their guns spoke, and redmen tumbled into the clouds of dust raised by their wild-eyed, terrified ponies' hoofs. But they came on. There was no stopping them.

When they were at the foot of the bluff, the defenders

leapt for their horses, and rode away.

Now it was a race after the wagons. Guns were emptied and at that speed they couldn't be reloaded. The Indians stopped their war screeches and held their breath for the struggle that was sure to come. The race was eerie, uncannily quiet, after the din of battle.

Soon they came in sight of the wagons crashing along. They hadn't far to go now, but the horses were just about spent and failing rapidly. And the Indians were coming up fast on their hardy ponies.

They were riding close in now, no more than a couple of dozen yards on either side of the compact, galloping bunch of cowboys and settlers, knowing there wasn't a gun loaded among the lot of them. Tombstone saw them drawing up, coming level, and flogged his gallant horse to a final endeavour. Just behind the two kids were clinging to him like leeches, determined to be at his side when the final showdown came.

The riders caught up with the wagon train just as the first one crashed over the descent by the cliff edge that bordered the plain on which the main body of wagons was situated. The half dozen men that were riding with them emptied their guns and for a moment that made the leading Indians swerve out. Then they were back, streaking in now towards the wagons.

The settlers fought them off with fists and knives, but more especially the swinging butts of their rifles. They would not yield an inch; they hurled themselves at the Indians to keep them away from the lurching, crashing wagons . . . and succeeded.

One Indian got through, a wild-eyed, naked fanatic. He took a flying leap off the back of his pony and clung to the canvas that covered the fourth wagon. A kid inside – a girl with plaits, about eleven or twelve – just put the barrel of a gun against the bulge in the canvas and pulled the trigger.

The first wagons were in sight of the settlers out on the plain beyond, but the Indians were almost in among the wagons now. Tombstone, hitting out madly at the copper-coloured faces, saw the greatest danger. A group of three Indians had cut ahead and were trying to turn the team on the leading wagon. If they succeeded, that brought the train to a stop, and if they stopped . . . That was the end to every woman and child in those wagons.

Tombstone went flat on the back of his horse, and the rowels of his spurs raked it as he had never spurred a horse before. . . .

Out on the plain they saw it happen. Blackie – the train captain – had brought every able-bodied man out a couple of hundred yards from the wagons, so as to give help as soon as possible to the desperately pressed party.

One minute they were looking at the empty trail that came abruptly down the break in the cliff. The next minute the leading wagon swayed over the top behind the sweat-stained panting horses – horses that were so near to dropping that only the lash of the long whip seemed to keep them up on their feet.

The first wagon . . . then the second, and with it came a flood of Indians and palefaces, spilling out onto the plain. Then the third wagon . . . the third wagon lurched so much it would have fallen, but a big, fair-haired man saw the danger and rode up, clinging to it until it settled on to its wheels again.

A long pause . . . then the fourth wagon, and the fifth.

But before this they saw Tombstone riding like fury to prevent the leading wagon from being turned. They saw the big cowboy deliberately charge his horse into the three fast-riding Indians . . . next second they were all down in a whirl of legs and arms. They saw Tombstone rise and pick up a gun and swing it, just as a bunch of Indians came screaming round him. The last they saw was of Tombstone fighting savagely, seemingly right in the middle of a solid bunch of redskins. But he bought those vital seconds that let the leading wagons race into the protection of the train boss's guns.

Then the fifth wagon came over the trail – it swayed, and this time there was no fair-haired man to swing on it and bring it back on its wheels. Over it went with a crash.

Blackie's men were firing, doing all they could from a distance to harass the braves. But they couldn't have saved the women and children. . . .

When the wagon crashed, every rider whirled his horse round and went leaping back. You didn't run away when women and children were in peril. Back they came, fighting their way through the screaming, milling Indians with berserk fury.

The two kids were first in. Corny came out with one child in his arms and another clinging behind him. Rip picked up the girl with the plaits and fought his way out . . . a big Lithuanian grabbed the woman and pulled her across his horse in a flurry of skirts.

The rest of the settlers ranged round the burdened horses . . . and then they were through.

That last wagon helped them. Every Indian wanted to be in on the plundering. They'd fought without reward or spoil for too long. Now they didn't intend to let some late-arriving Injun get their share of the white man's precious possessions.

The diversion gave the wagons and escort chance to get across the open plain to where a gap showed in the ring of wagons. All the settlers were streaming back now, with the Indians for the moment occupied in tearing the last wagon to pieces and in quarrelling over the spoil.

Mark Enty, wise to the ways of Indians, shouted, 'Who's the train boss?' Someone started a shout, 'Blackie!' and the black-browed train captain came running up. Enty held out his hand, and they gripped.

That was all. No thanks. It wasn't needed, and breath was better spent in other ways. Enty panted, 'These are Apaches, Blackie. I know 'em of old. Look, now they've sampled the loot there'll be nothin' ter hold 'em back. As sure as shot, they'll start another attack.'

Backie said, 'Wal? You got any ideas?'

Enty said, 'Yeah. They aren't expecting an attack. Git evry man across to shoot down as many as possible. Reckon we c'n kill a dozen or so before they know what's hit 'em. That'll knock the loot out of their minds, an' mebbe change their views on attackin' us.'

Blackie said, 'That sounds mighty good sense, pardner,' and then shouted to the men to come out from their positions inside the wagon train. When they were assembled, he told them what the plan was.

'We'll ride close, dismount, keep up as fast a fire as we can and drive 'em away from that wagon. But if they start a'comin', git back as quick as you can.'

The Indians were still fighting for the valuables in the wagon. Some saw the palefaces galloping near, but their warnings weren't heard by many of their comrades.

Two hundred yards away, the settlers slid to the ground and at once opened fire. Lead spanged among the braves, turning their savage elation into pain or – just nothing. So fierce and unexpected was the attack from the quite considerable body of settlers that, from the moment it was opened, the issue was never in doubt. The Indians had taken a mauling that day, and this was the finishing blow . . . They fled.

Enty said, 'We can forget them fer a long time now. We've taught 'em a lesson, I guess.'

Blackie said, quietly, 'Yeah, but look what it's cost us,' and then they rode into the circle of wagons. Blackie said, 'That's yore boy over thar,' – pointing.

Enty went over. A woman looked up from attending to the boy. 'You his paw?' she asked, talking down her nose as if she came from Connecticut or one of the Eastern states.

He nodded, his face lined with anxiety. 'How is he?'

She said, 'I don't know. He ain't come to, yet. He might pull round, or he might not. But one thing's sartin – ef you move him, he'll be a goner.'

Mark dropped on his knees beside the boy. She asked, 'Ain't he got no maw?' and Mark shook his head.

'She went a while back. That's why we're movin', I reckon.'

The two kids just fell from their horses when at last the opportunity came. The women were quickly round, bringing coffee and food. The yellow-haired girl sought them out. She held a can of coffee between the two of them.

'You're friends o' Tombstone, aren't you? Where is he? He ain't killed, is he?' She was concerned. The big puncher had saved her from the Indians only, it seemed, to die at their hands.

Then Tombstone came galloping in on an Indian pony, and flung himself down between them. 'Mine,' he said, grabbing for the coffee. 'I kinda need this.'

CHAPTER SEVEN

TWELVE THOUSAND DOLLARS

Then they all sat and looked at each other, until Rip said, 'The last I saw o' you, you were all down in a heap among a passel o' Injuns. I sure didn't give a dime fer yore chance o' makin' out, then. How come you got back?'

Farish was coming up. Tombstone said, casually, 'I heerd a bullet smack over my head. It knocked an Injun clean off his hoss, and as it came by I grabbed.'

'But the only thing he could ketch holt on was the hoss's tail, an' he came running out o' the ruckus hangin' on like grim death.' Farish stood grinning down at them. 'Never thought yore long legs could run so fast, Tombstone, pardner,' he chuckled.

Tombstone grinned and sprawled back gratefully, full length on the earth. 'That's the first time I ever came home on a hoss's tail,' he agreed. Then Farish squatted down.

'Feoder didn't come in,' he said abruptly.

Tombstone said, 'That's tough. I reckon we lost half a dozen men in that fight, an' we can't afford such heavy losses. How did it happen?'

Farish gulped from the coffee can. 'Reckon he couldn't stand the pace, after all. That shoulder must have hurt considerable, an' I think he jes' dropped back an' the Injun varmints pulled him down.'

They'd closed the gap in the ring of wagons now, and the wounded were receiving attention and the weapons were being cleaned and readied for any further attack, though Mark Enty said he didn't think they'd come again.

Enty called Tombstone and some other men across to confer with Blackie. Blackie put his point of view. 'It'd be safer ef we could get outa this country, away from these hyar Injuns,' he said. 'But we got some boys who mightn't stand up to travel. What do we do?'

They talked for a time, and then one old campaigner said, 'We ain't in a fit condition ter move. The hosses need rest, and that's a powerful argument why we should stay. I'd play fer Enty's hunch that the Injuns will have had enough.'

Blackie looked round. Most of the men nodded approval at this latter proposal, so Blackie rose, dusting his pants, and said, 'OK, we stay here fer another day, then. But I hope ter God you're right, Enty. We ain't in no condition now to withstand another attack.'

Tombstone and the boys saw the relief in Mark Enty's eyes. Staying gave his boy a chance to fight for life. As they walked away, Tombstone said, 'I think we'll slip out tonight an' shoot up a few more Injuns, jes ter make sure, shall we?'

The kids were tired, dog tired, but they knew it was sound tactics; it helped them all but especially young Enty.

They nodded. Blackie got half a dozen men to join them, and they went out around midnight, wearing moccasins and trailing long guns. They found the Indians encamped about three miles away. They were a ragged, disorderly little army, sullen and sore from the beatings they had taken that day. If there was anyone on guard, the small group of settlers didn't see them.

They poured rapid fire in among the braves, sleeping or talking around their camp fires. Probably they didn't kill many, in that poor light, but they must have wounded quite a few and they set the Indians back in panic. The Indians must have thought that a big attack was coming, and remembering the defeats of the day, a lot of them just mounted and rode away as rapidly as possible.

By morning there weren't enough left to be dangerous.

Tombstone and his tired little party didn't know this, but they had a pretty good idea that that would be the situation, and they crawled into their blankets with the feeling that they'd had a hard day's work, but had finished it off well.

Next day was spent in lazing around and resting. The horses, upon which the entire success of the expedition depended, were rubbed down and attended to for injuries. Looking at them, Tombstone shook his head. 'Some o' these critters ain't fit fer nuthin' but a bullet,' he declared. 'But I reckon they'll have ter do. God knows they're needed.'

Some of the men went scouting that day, and brought back good reports. All the Indians had withdrawn, and the nearest bunch was now encamped close on ten miles away. Blackie smiled with relief when he heard the news. 'Seems we c'n depend on you ter know Injun tactics, Enty,' he said. And then he said, 'I reckon we better stay here another couple o' days, at that rate, or even longer. Ef the Injuns have vamoosed, then we might as well stay hyar as farther along the trail, an' we do need rest.'

It suited everyone. Young Enty came out of his coma about noon that day. He didn't know anyone, and was very weak, but still that was a heartening sign. The next day he recognized his father, and then they knew he was on the road to recovery.

Tombstone and the boys went out hunting and found elk and deer, as well as fine big turkeys. The second time they rode out, the girl with the corn-yellow hair came galloping after them. Almost the first words that Rip spoke were, 'We cain't make up our minds about you, ma'am.'

'Oh?' said the girl. 'Meanin'?'

'Meanin' we all three seems struck on that corn-yaller hair o' yourn, ma'am, an' we ain't decided yet which one is ter have yer.'

The girl laughed. 'You young shaver, sparkin' up to a gal at yore age. Reckon you'd better wait till you're older.'

Tombstone drawled, 'Me, I'm a lot older.'

'Wal, you c'n wait, too,' she flashed. Then she added, ' 'Sides, cowboy, who'd want ter be called Mrs Tombstone?'

'OK,' said the puncher. 'I got other names, but no one ever uses 'em, so I kinda fergit I was christened Ed Reilly. I was born in Tombstone, Arizona, an' that name's stuck to me wherever I travel.'

'Here's someone else sticking to us,' said Corny suddenly. He pointed. Jup Farish had set off at a hard-gallop after them. Jup didn't leave them much alone around the camp. Maybe it was because they were the only men he knew, but sometimes the kids thought that there was something more to it than that.

He touched his hat to the girl, and said, 'Mind of I join you?'

The girl smiled, and Tombstone nodded agreeably.

'Sure, Jup, come right along. We jes' aim ter fill the pot, an' I reckon you c'n shoot as straight as any of us.'

They jogged along in silence for a while, until Rip said, 'You got our names, ma'am. Mebbe we c'n know yore handle.' Rip was mighty interested in the corn-haired gal.

Her eyes twinkled. 'Sure,' she said. 'Fair's my name, Miss Fair.'

'Aw, gee,' Rip exploded, 'who wants ter call a purty gal like you "miss"?' His brother began grinning at that, and so did Tombstone. Farish just listened, as if he had thoughts of his own which screened him from the humour.

'Wal, my friends call me Belle – Belle Fair,' she admitted.

'Say, that's a swell name,' said the kid, sparking at her unashamedly. 'You're a swell gal, Belle, altogether.'

Belle said, 'Jes' you watch yore tongue, boy,' but she was laughing. And she laughed more when she saw his face.

'Boy?' he said. 'Aw, what d'you want ter spoil things for, Belle? Cain't you see I'm sparkin' you, honey? I ain't no boy; I jes' arrived a year or two late.'

Belle threw back that corn-yellow hair of hers and laughed out loud. The kid and Tombstone joined in, but not Farish, and then, yelling like mad, they all raced for the soft green valley that marked the stream from which they drew their water. It mightn't be the best way to set off on a hunt, but it was cheerful, and this day they had recovered pretty much from the recent battle with the Indians and felt that all was right with the world.

Even indifferent success that morning didn't cloud their happiness. The sun was shining, they'd lost their stiffness and bruises, and each was good company for the others. Even Farish opened up and became talkatively reminiscent.

Tombstone said, 'You don't seem sorry to be away from

86

Dutch Maxie's outfit, Jup.'

Jup Farish leaned forward in the saddle and squirted brown tobacco juice expertly down a gopher hole. 'I ain't sorry. Dutch sure was pizen, like you said.'

'He sure was.' Tombstone's eyes were faraway. 'More'n even I thought at the time.'

Jup spoke, and Tombstone realized that the *hombre* was squinting sideways at him, watching his face. 'All the same, you boys sure gave him cause ter be riled.'

Something in the way he said it brought all three men's heads towards him with a jerk. Tombstone reined, and they all stopped. The big cowboy shoved back his battered hat and said, 'I keep feeling thar's more behind all this than we know. Mebbe you know more than we do 'bout things, Jup?'

Farish said, sourly, 'An' mebbe I don't.'

So Corny pushed forward. 'Wal, let's hear what you do know, anyway, Jup. Thar's a few things don't click, somehow, an' I've bin puzzlin' a lot over them.'

'Such as what?' There was a cynical grin on the cowboy's face that got the three bristling. He might have fought well by their side, this Jup Farish, but out of battle they didn't get on much with the fellar.

'Look, Jup, why did Maxie send you boys such a long way after us? An' why did you come, riskin' yore lives as you did? *Hombres* don't come trailin' a fellar into Injun country fer days on end jes' cause a boss a few hundred miles back has given the order.'

Jup Farish spat again, and there was contempt in the action. ' 'Tain't no good you guys playin' innocent. We knew what you'd done jest as well as you did yourselves.'

Tombstone came round in front of the *hombre*, his eyes were hostile. 'Farish,' he said 'you'd better talk – and not in riddles, either.'

The girl was startled and pulled her horse away. Only a minute before they had been a light-hearted party; now there was menace in the air, the smell of death.

Farish felt it, too, but he was no coward. He said, 'OK, what have you done with them twelve thousand dollars?' Tombstone looked at the boys and then turned back to the puncher. 'I don't get you, pardner. What twelve thousand dollars?'

'Aw, come off it,' jeered Farish. 'We all knew you took it. There was no one else could have done but you three.'

Tombstone's guns came out. He said, 'I've had enough of this, Farish. I don't know what you're sayin' an' I ain't pleased by the way you say it. All I c'n gather is that you're callin' me a thief. That it?'

Belle called, 'Put them guns away, Tombstone. We ain't gonna have no fighting a-tween ourselves.' She was a spunky, resolute girl, and would have come between the two principals in the drama but for someone getting in the way with his horse. It was Rip. Now was no time for soft play with girls; girls should keep out of fights between men.

Farish drawled, 'OK, I might as well talk. Though I guess thar ain't much you don't know ... Maxie had a load of money in the house. He'd got it when he sold the Paso range to that Easterner, Wimpeny. They were in hundred dollar bills drawn on the Schmidt and Toller bank, an' that means right good money.' He paused.

Tombstone didn't speak, but he looked grimmer than ever. There was no mistaking the implication behind Parish's remarks.

'Wal, one mornin' Dutch woke up to find that someone had broken in durin' the night an' got away with the bills. When you ganged up on him, that morning, I guess it was obvious who had done the job.'

Tombstone said, sharply, 'I don't remember ganging up

on anyone. Maxie came out an' pitched into Corny, an' we jes' nacherly took his side.'

Farish plainly didn't believe him. 'Thar was no one else could have done it. It was someone who knew the way about the place, someone who knew he had the bills.'

'There was plenty other critters on that ranch apart from we three,' said Tombstone icily. 'You could have done it, Farish. So could a lot o' other boys.'

'The only thing,' grinned Farish, 'was that we didn't seem in a hurry ter git away, like you fellars.'

Tombstone gave it up in disgust. Plainly Farish was sure that he and the boys were responsible, and nothing would shake the idea out of his head – nothing, anyway, that he could say.

'I understand a lot of things now,' he said curtly. 'But we didn't take the money, so don't let me hear you sayin' we did.'

'Sure, sure,' said Farish agreeably. 'Don't reckon I'll git my hands on any o' the money now. Maxie offered us a coupla hundred bucks apiece, ef we got his money back.'

'Good pay,' Tombstone nodded. 'Though I guess you didn't expect it to cause you as much trouble as it did – fer nothing.'

Farish gave his sour grin and said, 'I got a feeling I ain't popular now. Mebbe I'll find my own way back to camp,' and touching his hat politely to Belle he spurred his pony up the soft green slope and disappeared round a clump of elders.

That spoilt the atmosphere. Tombstone and the boys jogged on in moody silence, and Belle seemed uncertain what to say and so she kept quiet.

Rip, impatient and impetuous, got fed up after a while and broke the silence. He twisted in his saddle and looked across at Belle.

'Gal,' he said, 'ef it wasn't fer you, we wouldn't give a

hang what Farish thought about us. Reckon he ain't much good, anyway. But he said it in front of you, an' I guess we're all wanting ter know what's goin' on in yore mind in consequence.'

Tombstone whirled round. a little annoyed. 'Aw, kid,' he said, 'It ain't got nothin' ter do with Belle. Sure, Belle, now, you don't need ter say anything, ef you don't want to.'

Belle came out with a forthright, 'Did you boys take that *hombre*'s money?'

Tombstone reined. 'Belle, we never took his money. That's the first we knowed about it, what you heard jes' now.'

Corny said, just as quietly, 'That's right, Belle, you don't need ter start thinkin' you've met up with thieving mavericks. We never stole that money, an' we've never stolen any in our lives.'

Belle just looked at them, then her face cleared and a smile like the sun shining round cloudbanks lit up her face. She nodded, 'You don't need ter say no more,' she said. 'Reckon I'd take yore word afore that surly critter's any day.'

Tombstone's grim face relaxed. 'You're a good gal, Belle. Pity young Rip's sparkin' you or I'd go fer you myself.' With that, on an impulse he leaned forward and placed his hand on her strong brown one.

Belle twinkled, 'What's wrong in a gal havin' two strings to her bow?'

'What's wrong with me?' demanded Corny.

'OK, then. Three strings. I ain't never been as popular as this before. Guess it feels nice,' said Belle, and then she laughed aloud and the others joined in and that washed away the unpleasantness left by Jup Farish's accusation.

The wheels rolled the next day. Young Enty had come

along well and was able to be moved. He lay in the back of his father's wagon, and all day long people came to talk to him over the tail so that what might have been a bad and irksome journey for the lad was tolerable. He was a nice kid, and a brave fighter, and that made him popular with everyone.

For a week they travelled, and the going wasn't too bad. They saw traces of Indians, but they did not appear to be in force and so no one lost any sleep over them. The wounded were recovering, the horses seemed to have got their strength back, and all was right with the world. Increasingly, day by day, the conversation of the settlers turned to the land ahead that was to be theirs.

Good land, they had been told, and the guide who was taking them there said it was as good as any in America. His words were listened to with respect; he had lived in Southern California, even in the days when the land belonged to the Mexicans.

'It seems ter be a purty good place ter settle in,' said Tombstone. 'Nice, Spanish people, courteous and polite – haciendas and ranchos . . . cultivated gardens an' plenty of time fer leisure. Kinda makes me want ter git my feet in an' start raisin' cows o' my own.'

'Yeah?' said the young and cynical Rip. 'Mebbe you got ideas on raisin' more than cows. Couldn't be that Belle's attractin' you jest as much as Southern California?'

Tombstone said, 'Could be. She's a mighty fine gal, is Belle.'

'Wal, don't fergit you got competition. Me'n Corny got ideas 'bout that corn-yaller hair o' her'n. Ef you up an' marry her afore we know what's doin', we'll be powerful mad, won't we, brother?'

Corny said, 'So mad, guess we'll make her a widder right away.'

'Mebbe we'd better tell Belle what'll happen ef she takes a husband outa our family, Corny,' said Rip. 'Then mebbe she won't go an' make any mistakes calkilated ter bring trouble on poor ol' Tombstone hyar.'

Poor old Tombstone said, 'Ef you raise thet sorta conversation with the gal, I'll sure shoot the pants off'n yer. That sorta talk'd only embarrass her, I guess.'

'Embarrass Belle?' Both kids laughed outright. 'Sure now, thar ain't nothin' ter embarrass thet gal. Belle's the levellest gal I've ever met,' said Rip, and he made it sound as though he'd had considerable experience in his eighteen years.

Corny said, 'Mebbe he's afraid it might embarrass him,' and he looked at his kid brother as if there were possibilities in the thought. Rip looked back as if he'd seen them, too.

When you are grinding along slowly, day after day, you have to make your own fun, and the kids weren't backward in that respect.

They'd got into the habit of going over to Belle's wagon and having supper with her folks when camp was made. Her father was a silent man, but not unfriendly in his way; her mother had the same corn-yellow hair and cheerful manner, and her accent was that of Denmark, where she had been born. There were two other yellow-haired girls, though they weren't more than ten or twelve in age, and there was a kid brother of even younger years. But the children were mostly asleep by the time the three cowboys were finished with their camp duties and were able to come across for a couple of hours talk before they turned in.

It was pleasant, after the blistering heat of the day, and the acrid taste of the dust that rose and enveloped everyone and everything during the journey, and the awful monotony of those slow-turning, creaking wheels. They would lie out on the soft earth, with the darkness gathering comfortingly about them and the night breeze springing up to cool them after the sufferings of the hours before.

Conversation would drawl along, in keeping with their tired, relaxed mood. Then the kids would start sassing Belle and she would give back as good as she took. This night the kids started again.

Rip began it by saying, 'Belle, I guess I'm quit sparkin' yer.'

She said, 'Oh, why? I'm gonna be disappointed.'

Rip rolled on to his belly and sought for a grass that would take the place of the cigarette he was too lazy to roll. 'Wal, Belle, Corny an' I have done some talkin' about you. We reckon we're young enough ter find plenty gals fer ourselves, but we kinda think that Tombstone's gettin' on in years an' if he don't grab yer now, he ain't likely ter be gettin' hissel' a wife, ever. So Corny an' I are kinda withdrawin' from the competition.'

Tombstone was shocked. They could hear his breath come in, and then he started over to Rip, his face red.

'Why, you young Rip . . .' he began.

Belle caught his hand and halted him. She smiled up.

'Don't get too serious with yourself, cowboy. The kids are only teasin' yer.' She pulled, and slowly Tombstone came down beside her.

Corny said, 'Oh, heck. Did we go too far that time, Belle?'

Belle laughed that pleasant, ringing laugh of hers. 'Don't be silly. Mebbe you didn't go far enough.' She leaned back against Tombstone, smiling up at him in the half-light. 'Guess I'm gettin' pretty fond of Old Man Tombstone, only he don't never give me a chance ter say it.'

The puncher looked down at her, startled. Before he could say anything Belle's mother looked up from the sock she was knitting and said, 'Guess he is mighty slow at that, Belle. The way a gal's gotta do all the talking's quite somethin'. But yore paw was like that.' She sighed. 'He was so slow, reckon he'd still be a bachelor ef I hadn't of done the proposin' – an' me not knowin' the language!'

Her husband took his pipe out of his mouth and for about the first time that night he spoke. He said, 'Yeah, an' see where it got me, marryin'. Better look at me as an example, Tombstone.'

It was three days after this that the storm came, and with it . . . disaster.

CHAPTER EIGHT

MAROONED

They had a guide with them who had been in the Army which had fought first in Texas and then in California, when the American Government had annexed those countries from Mexico. He was a tough, tireless man, who had travelled these trails before and knew every inch of the way from the Atlantic to the Pacific, from the Mexican gulf up as far as Alaska and Hudson Bay.

So when he came riding up to Blackie, the train boss, early one morning and said, 'Look, boss, you'd better git them animals a-strainin' in thar collars,' they knew that there was need for it. He was no alarmist, that taciturn old man.

Blackie said, 'OK, Sam. Somep'n gonna happen, d'you reckon?'

Sam nodded back the way they had come. There were low clouds over the hills they had just traversed. He said, 'Thar's a storm comin'. These late spring storms are pretty violent, when they do come. Jest ahead o' us is a tributary o' the Colorado Rio, an' I'd like ter be across afore we feel the force o' this storm. Ef much water comes down from the hills, we mightn't be able ter use the ford for a week or more until the river goes down again.'

Blackie sent the word down the line, and the pace quickened. The speed they were going, they thought they'd make the river by early afternoon, but the rain caught up with them about midday and it slowed them. The horses had difficulty in keeping their feet, once the rain soaked into the loose soil of the trail, and towards the end of the journey the wagons were frequently bogged down and had to be manhandled out.

Blackie and the guide held frequent conferences as the afternoon wore on and evening came. The guide was disturbed – this rain was only the beginning of the storm, but even so it must be filling up the river rapidly. Already, in mid-afternoon, the guide wasn't sure if the ford would be negotiable. That would be a set-back to the party, for a week or ten days' halt to their progress would just about run them out of the food they had brought with them. The guide didn't reckon much to their chances of hunting meat in this bare stretch of country.

Whips cracked and men shouted, while steam rose from the backs of the horses as they struggled gallantly to keep the wheels a-rolling. The rain was hissing steadily down, soaking everything outside the thick, waterproof canvas of the covered wagons. No time was lost in halts for food, and the teamsters and outriders ate as they rode from whatever food the womenfolk were able to rustle up in those lurching uncomfortable wagons.

Just about the time they came out by the river, the first of the storm winds caught up with them. One moment the rain was falling in long, slanting lines; the next a cold gale came roaring over them, dashing the rain into their faces and almost toppling the heavy wagons over.

About this time the guide rode forward with a couple of

the men. They came back half an hour later with the news that the river was rising rapidly, but for the moment they were able to walk their horses across.

Blackie shouted to Mark Enty and a few of the wagon owners. 'Sam says we c'n still make a ford, ef nothin' goes wrong to delay us. Thar's a risk – that we might lose a wagon ef one gets caught in mid-stream when a storm wind blows. On the other hand, it might be even more disastrous ef we have to stay on this side o' the river until the flood water leaves it and enables us ter use the ford again. I say, let's try'n make it. What have you got ter say?'

Every man said, 'We'll take a chance on gettin' through.' Another squall hit them as they slithered down the bank to the river, and then the rain really came down – for a while it was torrential in violence. But it was the wind they were afraid of, not the rain. You can't get wetter than wet through, as Corny put it, when Belle called to him from a wagon and gave him something to eat.

They took the first wagon across without overmuch difficulty. Then the second one got through, and then a third. But it was slow work, for they daren't try and put more than one wagon through at a time at first, because the ford was narrow and they were afraid to run off into deeper water.

But the river was rising too rapidly, and at last Blackie had to take risks. If they went on, one at a time, the horses would be off their feet for the last few wagons. With a quarter of a mile of fast-running river to negotiate, that meant they would lose these wagons.

They got the women and children off and took them across behind the mounted men, because now it was too dangerous to try and ferry them over in the floating wagons.

Tombstone and a couple of settlers took off Belle's

mother and children. Tombstone said. 'Cain't take you this trip, Belle. Wait for me, an' I'll come for you.'

When he came back, all the wagons except three were on their way over. It was now nearly dark because of the low rain clouds and the weight of water that was falling on them. Someone got a fire going on the far bank so as to guide them across.

Tombstone said, 'No time ter lose, Belle. Climb up behind me an' hang on.'

He and the other men drove the first of the remaining teams into the water. Then the second plunged in, to be followed by the last wagon of all. By now, in spite of their weight, they were floating, and only the stabbing feet of the almost submerged horses kept them from drifting down with the current. The mounted men had got ropes on to the wagon stays on the up-stream side, and were desperately hauling the clumsy, rocking vehicles over the ford.

There were a few men holding the first two wagons straight, but only one man appeared to be holding on to the last wagon. Tombstone, over his thighs in water, heard a shout from the darkness behind and turned back into the driving rain.

The wagon was swinging, the one man being insufficient to hold it. Tombstone caught hold of the rope and that steadied the wagon. But they had to fight hard to pull the tail end back, so that there was no danger of the straining horses being pulled off their feet into deeper water, and that took time. The other wagons disappeared.

The wind was coming up cold again, and the rain hurt as it hit their exposed hands and faces. Tombstone shouted. 'I wish someone had taken you across, Belle. This ain't no place fer you.'

She shouted in his ear above the rising storm, 'Don't

worry about me. It's this wagon we've got to think about.'

Tombstone twisted his face close to hers, 'Belle, I don't think we c'n save it. I think we'd better let it go. This wind'll be a hurricane in jes' five minutes. We'd never git it across.'

He pulled in on the rope and drew near to the sodden figure that was trying to keep the gasping, half-swimming horses moving.

'Unhitch the bosses an' get across on their backs!' he shouted.

The rising wind screamed suddenly and drowned his voice. Tombstone saw the man still thrashing at the beasts and went in even closer. Again he shouted, and this time the man understood. Tombstone started to help, then found that it needed all his strength to keep the wagon from blowing like a sailing boat before the wind.

Somehow they got the pin out and the horses were relieved of the weight. Tombstone saw the teamster take a flying leap and gain the broad back of one of the horses, and then they disappeared from view among the white-headed waves whipped up by the wind. He held on for a second longer, to make sure that the other *hombre* was clear.

And that second's delay proved almost fatal to Tombstone and Belle. The other *hombre* had already let go and was swimming his horse after the teamster. A sudden squall hit the broad canvas of the wagon and started it on a mad career down the river. Tombstone still had the rope wrapped round his right hand; before he could release it he found himself plucked out of the saddle, Belle still clinging to his waist. Next moment they were both under water, fighting for their lives. What happened to the horse they never knew. Probably it got washed downstream and was drowned.

Tombstone could swim, but Belle had never learned. Tombstone found the girl struggling frantically, holding his arms and restricting his movements so that both were drowning rapidly. There was no time for niceties – he shoved out with the flat of his hand and Belle lost her grip on him. The cowboy caught her by that long yellow hair of hers and dragged her to the surface. She started to turn towards him again, on top, but he bellowed in her ear, 'Keep still, Belle, or we'll both drown!'

At that she either obeyed his instructions or lost consciousness. At any rate, when Tombstone's feet touched bottom, a few minutes later, he found a limp burden on his hands.

He slung her over his shoulder and staggered out on to the bank that they had so recently tried to leave. The rain pitched down in torrents at them, and he could hear it scalding the river into fury behind him.

He had to find shelter for them, but now it was so dark that he couldn't see a thing. When he'd got his breath, he staggered forward, head down against the rain. After a minute he walked into a thick bush, and he crawled under it, dragging the girl behind him. It wasn't much protection, but it did break some of the force of the wind and rain, and so it would have to do.

Belle was stirring as he pulled her into the poor shelter, and then she seemed to come to all at once. Tombstone felt her shivering and wrapped his arms around her.

'You all right, Belle?' he shouted.

'Sure I'm all right,' she called back gallantly. 'But I guess I lost my wavy curls in that little to-do.'

Then she started shivering as if she would never stop, and Tombstone could hear her teeth chattering. He wrapped his slicker round her, and lay between her and the storm, to give her as much protection as he could, but it wasn't much help. He felt worried for her, but there was nothing he could do until light came.

Belle said that that was the longest night that was ever made. But even the longest nights must end sometime, and this was no exception. Dawn came, cold and cheerless, and with it the storm temporarily subsided.

They stirred and sat up. They weren't much to look at, in that ghastly light, but at least they had enough left in them to be able to raise a grin. Belle even said, 'If I look like what I think I look like, then I guess it's goodbye ter my chances with any fellar.'

Tombstone put his arm round her and drawled, 'Honey, when yore as old as them kids say I am, you cain't pick an' choose. Reckon you'll have ter do for me.'

Belle said, 'Ef that's a proposal, you're pickin' a mighty queer time ter make it. Still, it'll do – Ed.' And that was the end of Tombstone so far as Belle was concerned.

Shivering, they stood up, and looked around them. The river had risen to within a couple of dozen yards of them, and now stretched, yellow with suspended soil, until it got lost in the curtain of steady falling rain. Behind them, sodden earth and drooping bushes dissolved into the same cold grey curtain. It was a depressing sight.

Tombstone said, 'We gotta find better shelter. C'mon, Belle.'

They stirred their stiffened limbs into a walk, and headed down stream so that the wind was to their backs. They first found a thick clump of aspens, and Tombstone left the girl there while he explored alone. She was feeling pretty weak, following the night's exposure, and Tombstone was already worrying about their lack of food and fire.

After a time he saw a rocky escarpment inland a little, so he turned to explore it, hoping to find a cave. The best he could find was an overhang which promised shelter because back of it the sand was still bone dry.

He went and fetched Belle, half-carrying her because she didn't seem to have any strength left. Then he went out into the rain and started to tear off some leafy branches from the trees nearby. He dragged them back to the overhang and piled them in a wall across one corner of it. As a windbreak it acted better than he had hoped.

Tombstone got Belle out of her slicker and made her lie down on the soft, dry sand. Then he covered her with his slicker as well as her own. He was scared by the pallor of her face. She must have drunk a lot of water last night, quite apart from shivering from exposure ever since. He wished he could get a fire going, but his matches were wet and he hadn't any tinder on him.

Then suddenly he got an idea. He collected dry kindling from the back of the overhang, and built it into a tiny heap, ready to be ignited. Then he took off his guns and ammunition belt and spread them out to dry on the sand. With his knife he got the powder out of two of his rounds of ammunition and placed it under the kindling.

Then he dried his revolver as well as he could and put one round in. Holding the revolver flat across the little heap of powder, so that the muzzle was touching it, he pulled the trigger.

The bullet thudded into the soft earth bank; the short spout of flame licked into the powder and ignited it. Tombstone flung his body across the front of the little fire, so as to prevent any stray draught from blowing it out. Carefully he built up the tiny flame until it caught on the twigs . . . and then they had warmth.

Tombstone built the fire until it was a large and roaring furnace, so hot that they had to sit back from it. Too hot – but for a while they revelled in it, after the cold misery of the night they had had.

Its effect on Belle was astonishing. In a short while the colour was back in her cheeks, and she was sitting up and talking again. But Tombstone didn't linger long over the fire, though. He caught up his slicker.

'I got an idea mebbe that wagon might ha' blown ashore downstream. Ef so we'll eat as well as keep warm. While I'm away, get your clothes dried out Belle.' Then he stepped out in to the rain that was coming down as hard as ever.

He found the wagon, as he'd expected, a couple of miles downstream. It had blown against a tree, half-fallen from a crumbling bank, and the canvas roof had hooked on to the point of a broken limb.

He had to wade chest deep to get into the wagon, and he found it awash with a couple of feet of water. A flour sack had burst, and everything was covered with slimy white paste.

He found a waterproof and wrapped into it some flour that was in a bag just out of reach of the water. Then he got a side of bacon, a sack of beans, some salt, coffee, and dried fruit. He salvaged some pans that were floating about, and then carried his load back to the overhang.

Belle's eyes lit up when she saw the success of his expedition. 'Now it can rain fer a fortnight,' she declared. 'We ain't gonna starve.'

She wanted him to get his clothes dried, but Tombstone said no, he had to go back to the wagon and get more things in case the rising river washed it beyond their reach. Especially they would need blankets, and he also had in mind the idea of cutting off a fair-sized piece of canvas to act as a tent for them.

It didn't take long for Belle to rustle some grub, and both sat down to big plates of steaming beans and bacon.

Tombstone had forgotten to look for spoons, so they had to use fingers, but as meals went it still was a great success.

When it was over, he put on his slicker again. 'I'll soon be back,' he said. She wanted to go with him, but he didn't see the sense in her getting wet, so he made her stay behind and tend to the precious fire.

He made three trips that day, before he was satisfied. By that time the overhang began to look like an Aladdin's cave to them, they had so many riches. The cowboy tried to rope the wagon to the tree, but next day when he went he found that, as he had expected, the rising river had torn it adrift and that was an end to the covered wagon that had come so far.

It rained steadily for the next three days, and it seemed that they lived in a tiny world all of their own, with the curtain of rain the limit to everything. The handy cowboy made them very snug – blankets had been thoroughly dried before the fire on that first afternoon, and he'd got off a good half of the canvas from the wagon, and that made a good tent for them. Night and day they kept the fire going, so that at all times they never lacked for warmth and cooked food. Without that fire and the treasures from the wagon, they both knew that they could not have survived. . . .

On the fifth day the rain slowly faded away, and then the mists began to rise as the hot sun warmed the wet earth. They came out of their camp and walked cautiously down the sodden hillside to the edge of the river. Now it seemed to be half a mile wide, and rolling strong with sullen, yellow flood water. They stared anxiously at the far bank, but it was deserted.

Tombstone said, 'Reckon they've given us up for lost,' but when they got back to camp the first thing he did was to carry some of the fire on to a small hillock and build it up with wet wood. 'Mebbe someone'll see the smoke an' know we're all right,' he said.

At first they just hung around the water's edge, hoping to see someone across the river, but that began to get boring and so Tombstone started to build a raft.

They'd need a raft if they were to get across the river. Belle couldn't swim, and anyway the current would be too strong and treacherous for many days before swimming became more than a suicidal effort.

He'd salvaged an axe from the wagon, and now he went to work steadily, chopping good-sized limbs from neighbouring trees. His idea was to make a raft with a platform on top so that they could keep well above any lapping waves. He also decided to fasten up a couple of short masts, between which he intended to spread the canvas so that it would act as a sail.

'That means that we're goin' to be hyar until the wind changes sufficiently to blow us across,' he explained. That could be a long time, but there was nothing else for it; no other way of crossing that swollen river.

Early that afternoon, as Belle was helping to roll logs down to the water's edge, they heard a faint call across the river. Instantly they turned and rushed to the brink,

'They've seen the smoke!' exclaimed Belle excitedly. On the farther shore stood a small group of people. Tombstone said he could make out the boys, and he thought that her father and mother were with them, and some other men. But the light still wasn't too good, with all the mist rising from the wet ground under the rays from the sun.

They tried shouting, but no word was distinguishable to the others, they guessed. 'Still, they know we're alive, and that's all that'll matter to them,' Belle said.

Tombstone stood on a slight promontory into the river,

making himself as clear as he could. Then he started signalling, punching his hand into the air and then spreading his arms wide.

'What're you doin'?' Belle asked.

'These are signals we use when we're out herdin' an' no one c'n hear a thing for them darned, bawlin' cows. I'm tellin' 'em to go on, we'll follow.'

'Think they'll understand?'

'Ef the kids c'n see me plain, they'll understand,' said Tombstone, straining to see across the yellow flood water. Then he whooped. 'That's Corny for sure, an' he knows what we're up to.'

Everyone seemed to be waving on the far shore, and then all but two of the party turned and galloped away. Tombstone said, 'It's the kids. Looks like they're gonna camp down until we git across. Then mebbe we'll ride after the wagons behind them. They're good boys, them kids.'

The only thing the boys hadn't reckoned on was the fact that they would have to cross the river by raft, and while the wind blew against them Belle and the cowboy were tied to this easterly shore.

Every day they came out from the overhang, hoping, but every day the wind still blew fresh in their faces, or blew not at all. Either was no use to them.

On the fourth day Tombstone said, 'Those kids must be gittin' short o' food. Ef they would leave one hoss an' git after the wagons it'd be jest as good as waitin' fer us.'

That morning he shouted until he attracted their attention. Then he again went through the signal to depart. They seemed to get it, but didn't seem to do anything for the next hour. Probably they were trying to work out the best plan of action. Then Tombstone and the girl heard them calling again.

This time the boys waved and then both mounted on to one horse and trotted inland. The other horse appeared to be tethered by a long rope close to the water's edge, where grass was thick and plentiful.

'Good boys,' approved Tombstone. 'They caught on fast, that time. Reckon we'll find they've cached some food for us, too, when we git across.'

The irony of it was that the wind relented the following afternoon, and started to blow across river. By now the current was less swift, and Tombstone decided that they could risk a crossing.

He launched the raft, then they hurriedly began to collect the food and equipment from the overhang. They took everything – 'just in case there was need for it on the farther bank,' said the cautious Tombstone. Then they pushed off. Once they were moving, Tombstone tied the canvas between the two short masts that he had fixed. At once the wind caught the crude sail, and they felt themselves moving out into the stream.

It was an uneventful journey. The big trouble was that they travelled so slowly that the current took them a good couple of miles downstream before they made the farther bank. Tombstone tied the raft securely, then carried everything ashore. He thought that all they would need would be food and blankets, for even under a double load, their horse should catch up with the wagons in about three or four days' time.

Then they tramped back to where the horse had been tethered. When they got there they found it was gone.

CHAPTER NINE

ON FOOT IN THE DESERT

Tombstone looked round to make sure they had come to the right spot, but there was no mistaking it. Here the ground was chopped up where the horses had been, and there was even the stake pin still driven in where the horse had been tethered.

The cowboy, his heart sinking, said, 'Somehow that rope musta come unstuck.' But he couldn't believe it. When cowboys tie knots, they don't came unstuck, and the kids were pretty smart cowboys.

Suddenly he found Belle close against him. She was gripping into his arm in shock. . . .

'Ed,' she whispered. 'Someone's watchin' us . . . from behind that scrub!'

He wheeled, his hands going for his guns. A man sat a horse back of the scrub, just as Belle said. He wasn't moving, just watching them.

Tombstone's guns streaked out, but the *hombre* was beyond range of them. He called, 'Hey, you, come out an' let's see yer face.'

The man rapped back, 'Stay where you are. Drop yore guns to the ground an' step away from 'em. I got a rifle hyar, an' I'll perforate yer hide if you don't jump to it!'

That was the second shock. 'It's Farish,' said Tombstone in wonder. 'Now, what's biting that *hombre*?'

A bullet suddenly screeched past his head. They saw Farish hurriedly reloading. 'The next one'll be your lot, Tombstone,' grated Farish. 'You're as good ter me dead as alive, I reckon.'

There was nothing else for it. Tombstone dropped his guns, then walked to one side. At that Farish cantered forward, holstering his rifle and drawing a six-shooter. Without further telling, Tombstone lifted his hands skywards. This Farish galoot was a mean man right now, by the sound of him.

When he came up, Tombstone said, 'What'n the hell's bitin' you?'

Farish answered simply, 'Twelve thousand dollars.'

Tombstone exploded, 'God in heaven, you still got that on yore mind?'

'Sure have.' Farish leaned forward in his saddle. 'I never did believe you when you said you didn't take the money, Tombstone. That's why I came back with Feoder, that day. I reckoned you had the money hidden somewhere close at hand, and I figgered ter git my mitts on it someday. Wal, I reckon that day's come. Hand over!'

Tombstone just stared for a second, then said, 'I reckon this sun's crazed you, Farish. I ain't got more'n thirty or forty dollars on me right now, an' they're silver ones – Mexican variety. But I ain't got no twelve thousand, and I never have had.'

Farish was getting nasty. 'You know what I said about your bein' dead? I gotta good mind ter drill you; I'd find the dollars without any trouble, then, I reckon. My guess is you've got the money – I guess you're more likely ter hold it than the kids. An' I guess at critical times, like we had last week, the first thing a fellar does when anything threatens is ter git the money from wherever it's bin hidden – say in one of the wagons – and stick it in his pocket or in a belt.'

Tombstone didn't say anything. He simply unbuckled his belt and slung it across to Farish; then he stripped off his shirt and threw that after the belt. Farish got down and examined belt and shirt. Within seconds he was satisfied that neither contained money.

The cowboy said, 'Farish, I ain't gonna take my pants off, not even fer you. But if you don't take my word for it, you'd better come an' give them the once over.'

They could see that Farish was worried and baffled now. He had been so sure that when Tombstone came across that river he would have the missing money on him. Now doubt was crawling into his suspicious mind . . . mebbe Tombstone was right and he didn't have the money.

He made Belle stand well back, and then he ordered Tombstone to turn, and he went cautiously up and examined the pants to see what was in the pockets. But he didn't find the twelve thousand dollars. Then he went across and threw everything out of the blankets, and made a thorough search of everything they had brought across with them. But still no twelve thousand dollars. He was baffled.

Then he said, 'Ef you haven't got them dollars, then the kids must got them. That or . . .' He turned his narrowed eyes towards Belle.

'Belle ain't got any dollars,' said Tombstone quickly, jumping forward a pace in spite of the threatening gun. 'I tell yer, I ain't never seen them twelve thousand dollars

110

you're all het up about. You keep yore hands off'n the gal.'

Belle said, surprisingly, 'Aw, shut up, Ed. You know even twelve thousand dollars ain't worth a hole in yore head.'

Tombstone's head came swinging round in surprise, and then it stopped and he became rigid. The lights came on again in Farish's eyes. He stepped forward, suddenly licking his lips.

'You got the money, Belle?'

She made her voice sound surly. 'See fer yerself,' she said, taking off her buckskin shirt. Then she threw it on to Farish's gun-hand.

The gun went off, and missed. Tombstone took a long flat dive and crashed Farish to the ground. Belle saw them fighting madly for the gun, saw Tombstone force it backwards – then it fired and she heard a high scream of pain.

She rushed across and picked up one of Tombstone's guns. He was fighting desperately, seeking to hold on to that gun arm, but that left his body exposed and suddenly Farish got his feet up and kicked him away. Both started to roll to their feet, Farish with his gun hand coming up. Tombstone started to dive, but he would have been too late. As it was, Farish was dead when he crashed into him.

Belle shot him. Tombstone got up, and went quickly across to her, not sure how she would take it. But she seemed calm enough, though maybe she wasn't quite as rosy under her tan as she normally was.

She just said, quietly. 'It ain't as bad as I thought, shootin' a fellar. Reckon it was you or him, Ed, an' I got a lot more use fer you than that critter.'

Tombstone just nodded, and put his arms round her for a second. Then he turned. 'Something screamed when he fired,' he said.

'It was his hoss. He got it in the shoulder. Reckon we'd better take a look at it.'

The cowboy said, 'You start lookin' fer the other hoss,' then went into a thicket where the beast was lying. Belle, climbing a hill, heard a muffled report from a six-shooter, and knew what had happened. Tombstone came with long strides after her.

'That was something I didn't like doing,' he said. 'But that horse was no good for anything, I reckon, an' I jes' put it out of its misery.'

Belle said, 'It won't be too bad, so long as we can find the other critter. Reckon we'll catch up with 'em in time, even ridin' double.'

They found the horse that the kids had left. It was Corny's, quite a big, strong roan. They rode it back to the river bank, and while Tombstone heaped stones over the dead Jup Farish, Belle sorted out what food and equipment they would need to take with them. Fortunately Farish had a water bottle and canvas war bag, and the kids had also left them a bottle and canvas sack. There was some food in it, but nothing much.

'Either they guessed we were doin' well fer food, or they didn't have much to leave,' Tombstone opined.

Then they mounted, took one look across the river at the overhang that had been their home for a week now, and plunged into the scrub.

After the recent rain this part of Arizona, which normally was a desert, seemed clean and fresh, and everywhere new plant life was miraculously bursting forth with greenness and flowers. It was like a lovely garden.

Soon they came to the wagon trail and settled down to a steady walk. After a while, to conserve the energy of their heavily laden horse, Tombstone dismounted and walked.

When the sun set, they halted and Tombstone made up a little fire and they had food and ate and then rolled into their blankets and went quickly to sleep.

Next morning they were up as soon as the sun, and once more they set off briskly. This day Tombstone walked all the time. He couldn't risk foundering the horse with his extra weight. Quite often Belle dismounted and walked with him, too, leaving their horse to carry only their blankets, cooking utensils and food. But Tombstone went too quickly for her, and soon tired her out.

It was hard going, though, under that torrid sun. Hour after hour they moved forward, drooping under its pitiless glare. Their faces peeled, and their eyelid's stuck together with the heat.

So when the sun was right overhead, he called a halt.

'Reckon we'll kill ourselves, ef we try'n go on in this heat,' he said. 'Guess it'd be better ef we did most of our travellin' during the night, though I ain't happy at the thought of losing the trail.'

He fixed a blanket across between two bushes, and gratefully they crawled into the shade and lay there, gasping as the heat rose from the desert, until the shadows were long. Then they made coffee – neither felt like eating – gave their horse some of their precious water – and started again.

Belle said, 'It must have bin just as tough fer them kids,' but Tombstone said no, not quite. They weren't their weight and had probably ridden much more of the way. Besides, the wagons couldn't have been more than a couple of days' ride away for the boys, so they could afford to press their horse a bit.

'We got farther ter go,' said Tombstone, and wondered how he could get water to help them.

In the cool of the night they plodded steadily forward. Belle dozed in the saddle, but Tombstone seemed tireless and kept right on leading the horse, hour after hour. He only halted when he was sure that they had lost the trail in the dark.

'We'll camp down fer the next coupla hours to dawn,' he said. 'When light comes we'll retrace our steps an' find the trail again.'

All too soon the sun rose upon another day of toil for them. That morning they finished their water, and had none for their patient horse. But the horse had found some green grass and so it wasn't as badly off as they. They got back on to the trail while the morning was still cool, and then walked and rode for six more hours before again seeking shelter from the sun. All the time Tombstone had been looking for water – and found none.

They didn't speak from the moment they halted until once more in the cool of the evening, they stirred their weary limbs into fresh activity. Tombstone thought, 'If we don't get water soon, it's the end.'

About midnight Belle suddenly reined the slow-moving horse. Tombstone was hanging on to the stirrup, nearly finished. Belle said, 'I c'n hear someone comin' down the trail.'

Tombstone said, 'You're imagining—' and then stood up straight. Someone was coming down the trail – more than one horseman.

Somehow strength came back into his limbs at that. He pulled the tired horse off the trail, so that it was hidden against the black of some scrub thorns.

'This might be friends,' he said grimly. 'But I'd hate ter give myself inter the bands of some Injuns, even now. I'm also told the Mexes don't go fer gringoes much either, an' we should be movin' into what used ter be Mexican terri-tory soon. . . .'

So they waited. The horsemen were galloping swiftly down towards them. Both strained their eyes to see, to distinguish – and then realized that it was too dark for them to see at all. Then they heard a voice, and at once Tombstone went jumping out, shouting.

It was Corny's voice, and his kid brother was with him!

The boys came wheeling back. Belle just fell into their arms and never said a word until they'd emptied half a bottle into her. Then she said, 'Now I'm goin' ter sleep, boys. Thanks fer comin'.' And she just lay back and went instantly into sleep.

Tombstone was all in, yet he held out a while. He drank then talked for a few minutes. The wagon train was all right and going well. Everyone seemed fit – even young Enty was walking round at halts. The boys had caught up with the wagons, then realized that Tombstone and the girl might not get across the river for days, and so they had started back with a spare horse and some large canvas bags for water. As it was, the wagon train was only a day's ride ahead, and they'd catch up with it in one day if they pressed hard.

Tombstone said, wearily, 'We ain't in a hurry. Let's take two days at it.' Then he suddenly sagged and slumped.

Corny said, 'Guess we'd better cover the bodies with a blanket an' keep the vultures off.'

Two days later they rode up to the wagon train at the midday halt. It was a joyous reunion. Belle's mother made such a fuss of Tombstone that he was positively embarrassed – and yet it was nice. They put Belle into bed in a wagon for a couple of days, because she hadn't any strength left after the ordeal, but Tombstone, though he was very stiff, was out in the saddle that same afternoon when they hit the trail again.

As they rode along, content, the three buddies talked. Tombstone told them in detail of their adventure, and their meeting with Farish. He didn't tell them that Belle had killed the *hombre*, for some reason, and they assumed that he, Tombstone, had done it.

Rip said, 'I reckon he got what was comin' to him. Wal, I guess that's the last we're gonna hear about them blamed dollars.'

Wherein he was wrong, very much wrong.

After what they had gone through, the next four hundred miles of their journey were uneventful. There was the long, painful crawl across the Mohave desert, and then they were into the cool mountains again.

One morning they awoke shivering, and knew they were near to their journey's end. A few hours later they were through a pass and descending the western slopes of the range. After a while they ran out on to a saddleback, and for the first time saw the country beyond . . . saw the blue Pacific Ocean in the far distance.

Two days later they were on the plains. Now they were in rich, cultivated country, among orchards and vineyards, with pleasant Spanish-styled architecture everywhere, and smiling, happy people welcoming them to their country. Only three years ago the Americans had come as conquerors to California, but for once the conquered had suffered little, if at all, at their hands. So they were, in the main, friendly hereabouts.

One morning, with the cool Pacific breeze blowing across to them, Blackie, the wagon boss, called them together. He spoke to them all.

'This,' he said, 'is our last day together. By this afternoon we shall have reached our journey's end, and we shall be parting, each to go to his own land. For most of us, our wagons will still be our homes for months to come, but probably today their wheels will turn for the last time. Well, these battered, stained old wagons have served us

116

well. May you find your new homes just as staunch!'

It was an unexpected speech, with more sentiment to it than anyone had thought the dark-browed Blackie capable. But no one cheered; there was no fuss. People just nodded and slowly went back to their wagons. And, in the moment that they had achieved success, paradoxically came sadness – there had been a comradeship on that journey, something priceless, and now it would be lost in the parting.

Tombstone and the boys felt particularly out of it. They'd started off for the gold-diggings in the northern part of California, and this was only part of their journey. They still had four hundred miles to go. . . .

They sat back of a wagon, talking a lot, before the day's move began. When mid-afternoon came, and the settlers had reached the land that had been bought for them, the wagons started to separate as each went to find the land that was his. For a time life and activity would be fairly communal, but from this moment their interests and lives would diverge. . . .

Tombstone found the Fairs looking over the land that was to be theirs, good land that they had bought for a dollar and a quarter an acre from the United States government. Tombstone said, 'Satisfied?' and Belle's father took out his pipe and said, 'Yeah. It's good, Tombstone. Reckon this land'll suit me.'

Belle was on the wagon tail with her mother, unloading things and putting them under the wagon. Tombstone and Belle's father went across to join them. Belle's father said, 'I reckon Tombstone's got something on his mind. Reckon we oughta lissen to him.'

The cowboy was uneasy and played with his hat. 'Wal,' he said, 'it looks like the party's breakin' up, don't it? You're hyar, an' hyar's whar you're stoppin'. But me an' the kids set off for the gold diggings at Sacramento, an' that's a tidy bit further on.'

Belle stopped unpacking at that and turned to look at him. One hand was plucking at the fringe on her shirt; anyone who didn't know her might have thought that she was nervous, suddenly.

'The boys don't want ter stay hyar; they're a rarin' ter make their fortunes in the gold fields. Wal, I figger that San Francisco an' Sacramento ain't no place fer kids like them, so I guess I'll jes' go along with 'em.'

You could see Belle go all white and rigid then, but Tombstone, a blundering man, didn't see it.

'You see, the way I look at it, I owe these kids a lot. I reckon that ef I see them settled down, they'll manage ter go on livin'. But it's a rough place, by all accounts, an' they're mighty impetuous youngsters. Anythin' might happen to 'em afore they found their feet.'

Belle said, 'What about me, Ed?'

'You?' Tombstone was startled. 'Why, sure I'll come back ter you, Belle, jest as soon as I see the kids won't come to no harm. That is, ef yore maw an' paw don't object ter me takin' you away from them.'

Belle's mother said, 'We've known fer a long time that you'll be takin' Belle some day, Ed. We kinda got used to the idea by now, I reckon. Mebbe I'll cry a bit when the time comes, but I guess that's how it always is.'

'Yeah,' said her father. 'I reckon it's always like this with daughters.'

Tombstone said, 'I'll not be longer than three months gone, ef I can help it. I guess you won't need me, anyways. Thar's plenty o' Mexican labour in the valley, they tell me. Mebbe when I come back I'll have the money ter buy cattle an' start ranchin' myself.'

Belle said, softly, 'I reckon you'll come back broke, Ed,

but it don't matter. Jes' come back. I'll be waitin'.

They lingered another three days, helping some of the settlers and testing their horses. Then one day they went back along the trail, waving goodbye to their friends as they passed each wagon. Belle rode with them for a couple of miles.

She said, 'I find it kinda hard, now, Ed, lettin' you go. Anything c'n happen to you. Take care of yourself – fer my sake.'

The boys rode on. Tombstone leaned across, his hands caressing that corn-yellow hair of hers. Then suddenly he kissed her and spurred on. Not until he was several hundred yards down the trail did he turn. She waved to him, and he knew that she was crying.

Just over a week later they rode into San Francisco. Two days after they arrived, they had to buy new saddles. Someone put a knife into theirs one night and tore them to shreds.

CHAPTER TEN

THE ROARING
FORTY-NINERS

Santa Fe had startled the cowboys, with the streets suddenly crowded with trekkers to the goldfields, but San Francisco – that was something beyond their imagination.

Just a year before, the entire population of the state of California had been no more than about fifty thousand people. Then a man named James W. Marshall, a builder of mills, had discovered gold, and set off the biggest gold rush in history.

At this moment people were pouring into the San Francisco area at the rate of nearly two thousand newcomers a week; within three years California's population was to jump to over 200,000.

As they neared San Francisco, the punchers found themselves walking the trail behind a surging, tramping horde that were, like themselves, bound for the diggings. They came afoot, most of them, carrying all their worldly possessions on their backs. Mostly they were poor men, tired of the frustration and toil of city life – they had thrown up everything in this mad gamble . . . it would be worth the dangers they had survived and the hardships still ahead of them, if they could but strike it rich. Every man who walked that trail was dreaming of the rich life he could live if he struck gold; every man was living happily ever after – in his dreams. For only a very few would those dreams come true.

The punchers rode down to the harbour area, coming in on the trail from the south as they did. Tombstone reined and looked into the crowded shipping lanes. Never had he seen so many ships in one place all at once. The kids had never seen any ships ever, so they just stared.

An old timer came rowing to some sea-stained steps close by them. He came stiffly ashore, a few dozen gleaming white fish strung with twine in his right hand.

Tombstone leaned forward in his saddle. 'Howdy, sailor. 'Frisco looks mighty busy ter me.'

The old seaman spat juice and said, contemptuously, 'It sure is. An' you ain't makin' it any less so.'

'I guess so,' drawled the big cowboy. 'An' I reckon it'll be difficult gettin' lodgin's; mebbe you c'n help us thar?'

'Nope; I cain't help yer, pardner. You gotta go and trust yer luck. Ef you get a room atween you you'll sure be lucky. An' ef you c'n afford what they'll ask fer rent, then you sure are a wealthy man an' got no right hyar anyway.'

'He kinda makes me feel cheerful,' the kid said to Corny.

Then the seaman told them something that they could hardly believe, yet later they found it to be true. Most of those ships in the harbour were either deserted or had so few crew that they couldn't leave port.

The madness – this gold-fever seemed to infect the seamen as they came into the harbour. Not for them further hard days before the mast, when they were here where, according to rumour, you had but to dip a basin into any stream in order to fill it with gold nuggets. Crews deserted *en masse*. The old seaman pointed out one ship that had come in that very morning.

'Officers as well as crew – every darned one of them, captain included – came over the side as soon as they dropped anchor, leavin' the passengers ter make thar own way ashore,' said the old man contemptuously. He looked at them, hard. 'You know what? I'll make more gold from my fishes than most people will from their digging.'

That didn't sound encouraging, after the long way they had come, but the cowboys didn't feel too depressed. Each knew that they had never really expected the good luck to find gold – they had come out of a sense of adventure . . . and to date they had had their fill.

They rode through the city, dazed by the excitement and bustle of the place. 'Frisco, in the year '49, was the noisiest, gariest, shootingest, rip-roaring place anywhere in the world.

Streets of flimsy frame buildings were mushrooming, as the speculators got going. Bars got bigger, brighter, noisier – and more and more expensive. Gambling houses flourished on the suckers who had come so far and won out, only now to lose to professional gamblers who would take the skin off their back, just about.

Men had walked the entire length of the continent to be in on this fabulous gold strike; others had sailed all the way round Cape Horn, or struggled across the isthmus at Panama and then taken ship northward. There were people who had heard the call in faraway Europe, even in Africa and Australia and farther places still.

So it was that, the toughest surviving, as always, San Francisco was a tough town, too tough even for the hardriding punchers from New Mexico.

Tombstone said it, as he watched the howling, brawling mob that surged ceaselessly through the streets. 'This place,' he drawled suddenly, 'don't seem clean. Looks ter me that thar's far too much pisen about – two-legged pisen.' They knew what he meant.

It took them a whole day to find accommodation, and even then they were lucky to get what was offered to them. They were passing a mean boarding house just as a toothless old man started to fix a card on the front door – 'Room to let.' They took the room without seeing it, they were so desperate for accommodation now. You can sleep out in the country, but not in the filthy streets of a town like 'Frisco in '49.

As they were going up the rickety steps, they had to wait while a body was brought down. Tombstone said, 'What happened?'

The gummy proprietor tied his trousers tighter with string and said, 'He blew his brains out. Guess that's how it takes 'em when they don't find gold. You're lucky; that's why you're gittin' his room.'

When he told them the rent – five dollars each a day – they told him he'd never blow his brains out, not while he had a goldmine in that one back room. The old man just cackled. He was doing well out of this gold strike, and wasn't bothered about public opinion.

There was a stable at the back, but Tombstone told them to take their harness and lock it in their room while they were out. He had no high opinion of the honesty of the people he had met so far.

Then they went to make enquiries about the gold fields. Vaguely they had thought that they would be here in San Francisco, or just outside the city, but they learned that the rich goldfield lay up the Sacramento Valley, and that was quite a journey round the bay and into the hills beyond.

Tombstone said, 'We'll stay over another day, to freshen up the hosses, then we'll hit the trail.'

Corny said, 'I got an idea already that I ain't gonna be a miner. However, I reckon we might as well go out to the diggings, havin' come so far to see 'em.'

They called at a saloon for a drink, but found it too noisy, too full of hilarious diggers celebrating a lucky strike, too full of lugubrious men who had failed again. . . .

They came out, as the light was failing, and stood under the new-lit lamps on the board walk. The street was packed with eager late arrivals, surging up and down in their quest for food and lodging. You could feel the excitement come up out of the crowd, so that it seemed to hit you like something solid. Most of these men had gold fever so bad, nothing in the world would ever cure them of it. Just a few, like the cowpunchers, seemed to hold on to their senses. 'I ain't seen many rich fellars since I bin hyar,' drawled Rip drily, 'but I seen more bums than I've ever seen in my life before. You know what – I reckon mebbe few people are goin' ter find gold after all.'

'An' we ain't gonna be among the fortunate ones, huh?' grinned his brother. The thought didn't worry them. Mebbe they didn't want success which might tie them down to this stark-crazy town . . . cow-herding out on the ranges looked better than this.

They started to move off, and just as they did so a slouching, thin-lipped *hombre* came out from a side alley. He saw them, gasped, and stepped quickly back into the shadow. The three punchers strolled slowly by without seeing him. He hesitated for a moment and then followed, but he kept his hand on the butt of his gun as if he knew how quick these men were on the draw.

Next day the punchers strolled out again, sightseeing. By midday they had had enough of the civilization that

San Francisco had to offer.

Tombstone said, 'Fer Pete's sake, let's get ter hell outa this place. It ain't good fer man nor beast. We'll ride up the Sacramento Valley; ef it don't look invitin', we'll light out fer the cattle country without any more delay. Yeah?'

'Yeah,' said the kids, and all three quickened their stride and went back to their boarding house.

When they came on to the landing, Tombstone halted, his hand on the door knob. He said, 'Reckon we don't need no key ter git in. Looks like someone's bin and leaned agin the door.'

The door swung open to his touch. The lock had been torn off, though it wouldn't have needed much force to achieve that end. The three went quickly inside. The room was in disorder. The mattress had been ripped and the straw shaken out; the bit of matting had been taken up from the floor, their war bags had been emptied and their blankets shaken out.

Then Tombstone saw the saddles. They had been ripped open, and just taken to pieces.

'What'n the—' gasped the cowboy.

They stared at the disorderly room. For a second Tombstone thought that it was the work of a madman or someone with a spite against them, and then an idea snapped into his brain.

'You know what this is?' The kids stared blankly at him. Tombstone said, simply, 'Twelve thousand dollars!'

'What's twelve thousand dollars gotta do with this?' asked Rip, but Corny understood – you could see that by his face.

'Don't you see, kid?' explained Tombstone. 'Someone's made a very thorough search of all our belongings. People only make such an intensive search when they are sure they're after something big. Wal, somehow that says twelve thousand dollars to me.'

'Can only be,' said Corny grimly. 'Somehow we can't seem ter shake off that accusation, can we? The more we protest, the more we are disbelieved. But how the heck's the news got across hyar ter Californy?'

Tombstone sat down on the edge of his board bed. 'Looks as though someone who knows us has seen us walkin' around the town. I guess they must ha' followed us hyar, mebbe last night. But who could it be?'

'Could be Blatt Wheddon or Nutty Din,' said Corny thoughtfully. 'Mebbe they didn't go back ter Dutch Maxie's but decided ter try thar luck in Californy themselves.'

'Could be anyone at Dutch Maxie's,' said Rip. 'Could even be Dutch Maxie hissel'. We've come a long way round, an' it's possible that someone from the ranch has bin hyar a week or more now.'

'Whoever it was,' said Tombstone rising, 'it means we spend our last dollars gettin' new saddles. Now we gotta ride. If only I could get my hands on the fellar. . . .'

By the time they had bought some very poor saddles, they were almost broke. The toothless old man tried to make them pay for the bust lock, but Tombstone just turned slowly and looked at him and the old man doddered away without pressing further. Tombstone could sometimes look a very grim and forbidding *hombre*. . . .

They took the trail round the bay, then lit out for the Sacramento diggings. They didn't know it, but they were followed to the edge of the city. When it was obvious which trail they were taking, the man who was shadowing them turned and hurried back into the lower quarters of the city. An hour later he came riding out, and this time he had company.

In the late afternoon the cowboys began to see

evidences of the gold hunt. Back from the bay and up the streams that fed into it, men worked, some at sluices they had built, others with pans and cradles. Inland, men were digging, like worms casting their spoil all around them. It made the landscape wretched and desolate, with all those little hillocks of fresh-thrown earth.

But the Sacramento Valley, where the principal diggings were, was still a good distance off. They wouldn't reach the main field until the morning.

They jogged on until nearly sunset, and then they halted, not far from a shack town of a few dozen primitive buildings. Out here, they didn't need a roof over their heads for the night – here there was room for them to spread their blankets. Over a little fire they cooked their supper, then they decided to ride down to the saloon and try and get the latest news on the gold strikes.

The saloon was a cruder, dirtier, smaller edition of the vice palaces across in 'Frisco, But if anything it was noisier. The men in it were soiled yellow, just as they had come out of the diggings. And digging, that hot summer day, had made them thirsty, and almost every man-jack was riotously drunk when the punchers entered.

The bar was wet with liquor. Thinking of their depleted purses, they ordered the cheap tequila, then stood by, listening for any news that might have value to them. After a while a dried up old man came over and said, 'How 'bout standin' a fellar a drink, pards? Guess I'm right down on my luck.'

'Sure,' drawled Tombstone. 'Make it tequilla, though; guess we ain't seen much gold, either.'

The old man nodded agreeably. A drink was a drink to him, so long as it contained alcohol. He said, 'I don't reckon many people hev seen gold, come to that. Reckon thar's more talk than gold, when all's said an' done. Sure, a few fellars has struck lucky and got thar bonanzas, but not many.'

'What we heard,' said Tombstone humorously, 'was that every man jack o' you was makin' yore fortunes.'

'Sure, I heard them tales,' said the old man. 'That's what brought me hyar. That an' a wife.'

'Yore wife came with you?' They were surprised. They'd hardly seen a woman since they came to California. He shook his head, decisively.

'No, sir. I came to Californy ter get away from her. Couldn't stand her tongue any longer. Reckon a lot o' these men hyar has come ter git away from their wives.'

Just then there was an outburst of raucous song from a wild-looking group of harum scarums back by the bar. The shack rocked with the sound of their powerful, drunken voices. The old man said, 'They got a lot ter sing about. A man's lucky ef he gets a claim that pans him six or eight dollars a day.'

Rip sighed humorously. 'Reckon we'd better fergit this gold-hunt o' ours, boys. From all accounts, we don't stand much chance o' makin' our pile out hyar. Pity, I'd sure like a ranch o' my own.'

Another group of men had come through the batwing doors, only these weren't drunk.

Tombstone knocked back his drink, 'You don't think much to our chances, old timer?'

'Ef I was you, I'd light out termorrow,' said the old man earnestly. 'Thar's only sorrow an' sufferin' ef you stay around hyar, boys.'

He was a kindly old man, and well-meaning. Tombstone was just turning to order him another tequilla, when a loud voice rang out from the doorway.

'Don't move – 'cept ter put yore hands up!'

Tombstone's head came round quickly. Three men

were standing in the doorway, squat, tough-looking *hombres*, with guns pointing steadily in front of them.

Rip said, 'It's a hold up,' and then saw that the guns seemed to be pointing only at himself. Corny and Tombstone were suddenly thinking the same – that those guns were pointing in their direction. . . .

'You three at the bar,' rapped the *hombre*. 'Git them hands up.'

'Us?' Tombstone reluctantly reached towards the blackened ceiling. 'What'n the heck for?'

'I'm a United States marshal,' said the *hombre* impressively. 'You're under arrest.'

Everyone in the room was silent as the three men came slowly across the floor, guns never moving away from the punchers. Until suddenly Rip demanded, 'What are you arrestin' us for? We ain't done nothin'.'

'No?' the marshall sneered. 'Only took twelve thousand dollars, didn't you?'

'What?' roared Tombstone. Here it came again! Someone else was on to this story of the missing twelve thousand! 'Goldarn it, we never took any pesky dollars. Now I wish ter God we had!'

'Yeah? Tell that to the judge,' said the *hombre* meanly.

Unexpectedly there was a diversion. One of the wild-looking harum-scarums had turned; in his eyes was the light of Irish devilry.

'Aw, sure now an' it's the truth they're tellin' ye,' he said. 'Sure now, an' they didn't take the money at all, at all.'

'Didn't they?' asked the marshall sourly. 'I s'pose you know who did?'

'Why sure.' There was no hint of humour on that good tempered, Irish face. 'Sure now, an' we all took it, didn't we, bhoys?'

'Why, sure we did,' said the boys, a couple of dozen of

them. They started to move forward, and the marshal and his assistants suddenly grew uneasy. Irishmen were notoriously agin the law, and with some drink behind their belts, anything could happen.

Suddenly the entire bar took to the humour of the thing. It was the sort of rough humour that appealed to these men, many of them outcasts themselves. All in one second that Irishman had the entire occupants of that saloon protesting to the marshal that they had pinched the missing twelve thousand dollars. They started to crowd round the Law, unheeding the guns.

The Irishman who had inspired the affair slipped across to Tombstone and said, 'Git out the back way, while we fool the divils for ye.'

Tombstone said, 'You're a pal. If thar's anythin' I c'n ever do fer you—'

'Jes' cut me in on that twelve thousan' an' say no more,' said the Irishman.

'Damn!' exploded Tombstone. 'Another one thinks we got the money.'

Then a wave of happy, blarneying Irishmen formed a barrier between the marshal and the men he was after, and Tombstone grabbed the kids and bolted the back way. A minute later they were galloping out of town again.

Rip said, 'Say, Tombstone, what does this make us? Outlaws?'

The big cowboy said, 'I ain't stoppin' ter ask questions. I don't reckon ter stay in these parts, anyway. Me, I'm goin' back to my Belle jes' as soon as I've herded you boys on ter safer campin' grounds. An' I hope nobody down San Bernardino way'll start connectin' me with any missin' twelve thousand dollars!'

Rip said, 'Don't you be so sure,' and then reined suddenly.

Darkness had fallen now. They had come to the edge of this rough, useless lot of land on which the tiny town was built. Now the trail led alongside the river, and the beginning of the rich gold field.

By day they would have seen that every square inch of land from both banks of the river outwards was staked out and being worked. They would have seen rectangular claims some merely marked out with pegs, others roped off, others – where rich strikes had been made – fenced off or even barricaded. And on all grew the clay yellow subsoil hillocks from the diggings.

On nearly every plot stood some form of rude habitation – sometimes it was a frame with an old tarpaulin or sheet dropped over it; sometimes it was some shapeless thing made out of tree branches; sometimes a tent, and occasionally even a small shed.

Men didn't dare leave their claims, for all they had been registered and filed so, though conditions of life were appalling, they lived and ate and slept on their small, precious plots of land.

That was the scene by day. By night, under a moonless sky, all you saw as far as the eye could reach up that long, winding valley were the yellow lights from lamps and candles, and the reflecting redder gleams of firelight in the brawling river.

The sight was fantastic, and the three punchers stopped to stare at it. Then Tombstone said, 'Reckon we'd better pull in hyar, afore we git among them claims. Don't reckon we'll find much space to sleep on, once we move into that gold territory.' They'd heard that once the claims started, there was no spare ground for late-comers. Even the miners had to cross each others' claims to get to their own workings.

Rip had already slipped from his saddle, and

Tombstone was about to climb down, when they heard sounds behind them.

Tombstone said, 'Damn, I didn't think anyone'd follow on a night as black as this.'

But they were being followed. What's more, it soon seemed that the entire saloon was now against them and were intent on herding them down.

Round the bend behind them a flood of dark shapes came pouring into view. A few were mounted, but most came afoot. They were shouting, and there was ugly threat in their rough, angry voices. Some carried torches, and by the light from the flaming rope ends they could see faces – and the faces didn't look at all friendly.

Tombstone settled back in his saddle. 'Looks like that marshal's made friends,' he said. 'C'mon, Rip; we gotta ride.'

They started up through the claims, passing the fires and lamps of the miners – in two or three places men were still working by lamplight, but mostly they could see them resting and sleeping under their primitive shelters.

They rode up between the claims, along the narrow track that alone was left unworked. Then the flood of pursuers reached the first of the workings. They weren't too far ahead to hear what happened.

The miners woke up and stood to with any weapons they had. They didn't know the meaning of this horde that was coming upon them and they weren't taking any chances.

The punchers, quickening their pace, heard someone call from one of the claims— 'Hey, what's all the fuss about?'

And then, very clearly, someone shouted back, 'Thar's some claim-jumpers out ternight. They've got away with twelve thousand dollars in gold from one claim, an' thar's a marshal hyar after them.'

Claim jumpers! The words went like lightning along that valley bottom. Claim jumpers – the lowest type of criminals in the eyes of these hard-working miners. It ranked as low as horse-thieving among cow punchers, and that was as low as you could get.

It meant a rope if you were caught at it, and they didn't bother about trials in these parts.

More men joined the pursuers, more torches lifted and burned and illuminated the angry faces of the mob that was after them.

Tombstone said, 'We gotta keep ahead o' these *hombres*. Reckon they'll jes' string us on the word o' that marshal ef they catch holt on us.'

They raised their horses into a gallop. Already disturbed, other miners got up to watch the three black shadows gallop past.

Corny suddenly shouted, 'Tombstone, I don't reckon that fellar is a marshal.'

'Yeah? How come, son?'

'No marshal I have ever met would enlist the aid of a mob by putting across a phoney story. Marshals like ter git thar men, but they like 'em alive. We'd be no good to the marshal hangin' from a tree.'

Tombstone said, 'Mebbe you're right, Corny. But what difference does it make? I'm gonna keep right ahead o' them so-and-so's!'

A few minutes later he began to think that mebbe they wouldn't be able to keep ahead. The trouble was, sound could travel faster than they, and now the words 'claim-jumper' were catching up with them as they galloped.

Men were relaying the call, and it was overtaking them – soon it would pass them. And then they would find their way barred by angry, armed miners.

Tombstone dropped his horse to a walk. Just here a huge rock outcrop kept the diggings well away from the track. The nearest lamps and fires were a couple of hundred yards away.

Tombstone said, 'Hold my hoss, boys.' He proceeded to swing out of his saddle.

Corny was startled. 'What're you goin' ter do, Tombstone?'

The big cowboy said, tight-lipped, 'We can't ride outa this. So I'm goin' ter try an' create a diversion. You boys hole up hyar until things quieten, then walk yore hosses quietly up the valley. I'll git after you, somehow.'

'What're you goin' ter do?'

Tombstone said, 'Right now, I don't know. But I gotta think o' somethin' or we'll all be dead meat.'

The wave of sound caught up with them then, and went surging around the big bluff of rock through which the trail crawled. It was too late now for them to ride any further, as Tombstone said, if they rode on now they would find their way barred by trigger-touchy miners ahead.

Tombstone ran swiftly, quietly, back along the trail. When he came round the outcrop he could see the advancing horde about half a mile behind . . . he could see men standing ready on their lamplit claims as far as sight would travel. They would get short shrift from these men, as claim jumpers.

Tombstone hesitated, then suddenly went boldly down the trail. As he walked he shouted, 'What'n the heck's the noise about?' and men answered, 'Thar's claim-jumpers out ternight. You'd better git back ter your claim; pardner.'

'I got pardners,' shouted Tombstone, 'Reckon they c'n look after the claim fer me. All I want is ter meet up with these blamed claim-jumpers – the varmints!'

It was a kind of password, talking like this. No one suspected him as he walked quickly down towards the oncoming mob – that was the last thing anyone would have expected of a hunted man.

Then fortune favoured him. Several other eager young miners, anxious to be in at the kill, left their claims and joined him. By the time they joined up with the mob, they must have numbered a dozen or twenty. They provided a screen for Tombstone, and he passed unrecognized.

But time was short. Now they weren't much more than a quarter of a mile from where the boys and the horses were holed up. In a few minutes they would be discovered. . . .

Tombstone racked his brain desperately, trying to think of some way of stopping that huge, ever-growing mob. He had to think of something . . . something quick . . . Something to stop them from going any farther. . . .

By now he had dropped to the back of the mob. Several horsemen brought up the rear, unable to ride through. Tombstone peered up at them, a sudden suspicion in his mind that these might be the marshal and his friends. But it was too dark for him to see.

Suddenly the idea came to him. He acted at once. There were about half a dozen horsemen, and the last rider was a few yards to the rear of the bunch.

Tombstone suddenly reached up and grabbed him. The fellow hit the ground with only a frantic gasp of surprise. Tombstone didn't like doing it, but three lives were at stake. He bumped the fellow's head with the butt of his gun, and the man sighed and went out like a light.

It was all done in a second. The startled horse was grabbed by the bridle and turned before it knew it had lost its rider. Tombstone pulled its head towards the claims, then slapped it heavily on the rump. The horse squealed and plunged off the trail. Tombstone's heavy gun roared in its ear, startling it even further. It panicked and went crazy.

Tombstone stood in the middle of the track, blazing into the sky and shouting, 'Thar they go! After 'em boys!' The mob stopped and turned. They could hear something heavy crashing up the hillside, could hear the startled, angry shouts of miners as the horse knocked into their tents and huts and sent them flying.

By the way those miners on the hillside shouted, you would have thought there was an army passing through, and that was pretty convincing to the suddenly halted mob.

'Thar they go!' the cry was taken up. Instantly the hotheads plunged up the hillside in the general direction of the noise. At once they got into trouble.

The miners had heard the shout, 'Claim-jumpers!' When they saw men jumping on to their claims they thought that this must be part of the claim-jumping plan. Instantly angry shouts rose from them and guns blatted and pick-shafts came swinging round. In no time there was a brawl of tremendous size going on by the side of the trail.

Tombstone had hoped to create a diversion, but he had never expected success like this!

He found himself alone, on the trail, except for some of the horsemen, who wouldn't risk their beasts out in the darkness. He thought, 'Now's the time. Ef I slip through, we three can come walkin' back an' no one'll ever be the wiser. Reckon mebbe after this we'd better fergit goldmining. Mebbe we'd better leave Sacramento to others an' git back ter herdin' dogies.'

He turned. It was disappointing. Back of his mind he'd all along had the thought that he'd like to make a strike, so that he could go back triumphant to his girl and buy a ranch and set up a nice house. That's the way a fellar likes to go back to his girl . . . not with his pockets empty. Still, going back with empty pockets was better than hanging out on the cold night breeze at the end of a rope, and he knew that sooner or later that fate would meet up with them, now they had been branded as claim-jumpers. . . .

Someone bent from a saddle and slugged him with something heavy. He passed out instantly.

CHAPTER ELEVEN

TOMBSTONE MEETS WITH TROUBLE

The big cowboy wasn't long unconscious; probably no more than three or four seconds elapsed before he began to come round. His head throbbing, he became aware of men stooping over him, a lucifer striking and casting a spluttering flame across his face.

Then a voice, satisfied, 'That's him. I knew I wasn't mistaken, even in the dark.'

That voice – where had he heard it before? It was familiar, but for the life of him he couldn't place it.

Someone said, quickly, quietly, 'Tie him – an' gag him.' Then rough hands were passing a rope around him and gagging him. He felt himself being hoisted across the back of a horse, and then someone swung up behind him.

That familiar voice queried, 'Now, where?'

A rough, growling voice answered. It sounded like the marshal's, to Tombstone. 'Back towards the town. I got a shack thar. It'll be safe enough. . . .'

Someone said, 'Reckon Bridgy's gone after them kids, the fool.'

Then the horse moved and they went walking quickly back down the trail. In a few minutes the noise of the fighting that had been going on all the time receded and finally faded.

Hanging across that horse, bound and gagged and face downwards, wasn't conducive to clear thinking. Besides, his head ached abominably where the gun had hit him, so he didn't make much sense of what had happened.

What puzzled him was, though the marshal and his friends had enlisted the aid of the miners to pursue them – a clever move, and he gave them full credit for the inspiration of 'claim-jumpers' – when they did spot him they had quietly smuggled him out of reach of the avenging horde. Now they appeared very anxious to get him away without any of the mob knowing about him.

Tombstone kept saying, 'Why?' but got no further than that question. He let himself go, no longer thinking, just trying to ease the pain in his head. It was rank bad luck that he should have been caught, just when he had turned the tables so neatly on their murderous pursuers. He wondered what the boys would do now, without him. . . .

Sometime later they halted. There was a creaking of saddle leather as men dismounted, a door was slammed open, and then a lamp burned up, giving an astonishing amount of light to their dark-atuned eyes.

Tombstone found himself hauled off the horse and dragged, heels trailing, into the pool of lamplight. He was dumped with his back against a wall.

It was a very small hut they were in. Three walls were occupied by double-tier wooden bunks; the fourth, against which he was lying, contained the door and there was also a packing case against it that seemed to be a table. On it was a lamp. A couple of splintery boxes seemed to be the only 'chairs' that the place possessed.

But Tombstone wasn't interested in the furniture. He was trying to see the faces of these men who had captured him. For a moment they were all dark shadows, as they milled in front of the lamp, then one of the men faced the light and he saw his face. It was one of the 'posse' that had held them up in the saloon. Then another turned – the 'marshal'.

Tombstone now was sure that Corny was right. This *hombre* was no marshal. But that didn't make him any less formidable.

There were five men in the room. Tombstone recognized the third member of the 'posse'. A fourth man came into view, a stranger, but no less tough-looking, no less evil with unshaven jowl and matted hair.

Tombstone tried to see the face of the fifth man, but he was to one side, sitting on a bed and so in the shadow from the tumbled blankets overhead.

Again this man spoke, and again Tombstone knew that he had heard that voice before.

'Reckon we'd better git ter work on him, fellars. Ef he won't open up, reckon we might have ter go fer them kid's again, an' now they might be miles away.'

That voice! It was irritating. Tombstone knew that he had heard it before, but just couldn't remember where. And he felt that if only he could see the *hombre*'s face he might be able to understand a lot of things.

But the fellar just sat there in the shadow. Maybe it was accident – perhaps it was by design that he kept his face hidden. . . .

The other four men crowded round the big cowboy. The 'marshal' hoisted him to his feet, so that he stood stiffly leaned against the wall. Tombstone saw that evil, bearded face within inches of his own. The fellar had slat eyes, narrowed and hostile; Tombstone didn't expect much mercy from a *hombre* with eyes as mean as his.

The marshal said, 'You got a choice, buddy. You c'n open up now an' tell us what we want ter know, or you c'n wait and take a whale of a pastin' afore you open up. But you're gonna talk,' he ground out savagely, and suddenly he reached forward and grabbed Tombstone by the shirt collar and shook him. Tombstone took it, because he couldn't do anything else but take it.

When the 'marshal' was through with his rough stuff, the big cowboy said, 'All this is fer what?'

'It's fer you ter recognize that you're fer trouble ef you don't tell us whar you've got them dollars hid.'

'The twelve thousand dollars?' Tombstone's lip curled ironically.

'Yeah, the twelve thousand dollars. You got 'em some-where, an' we aim ter git 'em off you.'

'So's you c'n give 'em back ter their lawful owner?' Tombstone jeered. He was playing for time. Even minutes might count . . . though how they might count he hadn't the faintest idea. He seemed to be in a mess, and he could-n't see any way out of it.

From the back shadows that voice spoke again, irritat-ingly familiar. 'Dutch Maxie don't need no dollars whar he's gone. An' he didn't leave no heirs. That kind don't.'

'Maxie? He's dead?' asked Tombstone quickly. 'How d'you know?'

'One of his boys came ridin' in last week. Said the outfit was bust up. Maxie got ter bawlin' out some stranger. Then the fellar went for his gun, Maxie went for his. But Maxie had fergotten that thar was somethin' wrong with his trig-ger finger, an' it made him slow.'

'Seems like I killed Dutch, then,' said Tombstone softly.

That startled the *hombre*. Suddenly he was on his feet and in front of Tombstone. And then the cowboy knew why the voice was familiar.

It was Scaramouch!

'You!' he said contemptuously. 'You got the story of the twelve thousand dollars from Dutch Maxie's man when he came in last week, huh? You saw me an' thought mebbe you'd earn more money outa me than by gold-minin', so you set these thugs on to me.'

The marshal growled an oath and struck the cowboy across the face. That didn't make his sore head feel any better.

Scaramouch said, 'Hold it!' his thin face perplexed.

'What did yer mean by that – that you killed Maxie? Maxie didn't die until you were half-way across the continent.'

Tombstone grinned drily. 'I still reckon I killed him, even from five hundred miles away. I kicked his hand an' broke his fingers, an' I reckon that's why the other *hombre* got his gun out first. An' good luck ter the galoot, whoever was.'

'Oh, that's the answer.' Scaramouch shrugged his shoulders at the simple explanation. Then Tombstone came back with a question, because now an idea had fired his brain.

'What's happened to the T-over-X?'

Scaramouch said, 'It's bust up. When Maxie went, everyone grabbed what they could and lit out. He'd got no real claim for most of his land, anyway; he hadn't never paid fer it.'

The 'marshal' was getting impatient. 'What the hell's that got ter do with him?' he rapped, shoving Scaramouch away. The way he treated Scaramouch, Tombstone got the idea that he didn't think much of the rat. And Scaramouch didn't like it either, being shoved around. He snarled something, and the brutal 'marshal' came whipping round, his manner threatening. Scaramouch muttered and turned away.

'Reckon maybe he's feelin' sorry he got these tough babies ter jine him,' thought Tombstone ironically. That was just like Scaramouch, to get someone to do his dirty work and then find himself frozen out of the spoils in the end. Tombstone didn't have much opinion of the thin-faced *hombre* and never had.

But there were other thoughts in his mind, too. Inwardly he was racing with excitement. Now he was beginning to understand a lot that had been mystery before.

Now, suddenly, he knew where those twelve thousand dollars were hidden!

Desperately he looked round that rough little shack, trying to see some way of escape. 'I jes' gotta get outa hyar,' he told himself, working unavailingly at the bonds round his wrists.

Yes, if only he could get away he could see those twelve thousand dollars in his hands – divided three ways it still meant that he'd be able to buy a small ranch of a couple of thousand acres down in that lovely South California cattle country, and he'd have enough to start a good-sized herd of Texas longhorns. In his mind's eye he was working things out, thinking that he could start with maybe four or five hundred cattle, and within five years he'd have as many thousand. . . .

Then the 'marshal' smacked him on the face again, jerking his head back. So Tombstone bent quickly, too quickly for the 'marshal', and the big cowboy felt the other *hombre*'s teeth as his head butted into that evil, bearded face.

The 'marshal' went back, lips split and his nose trickling blood, his eyes streaming with the pain of the concussion. ' You— You—' he snarled, and then he came back to hit the cowboy again.

Tombstone let his knees go and slid down the wall, just as that fist came swinging over, so that the 'marshal' hit the boards with a resounding thump.

All the same, Tombstone would have taken a beating but for the intervention of one of the 'posse'. This fellar, just as rough-looking as the 'marshal', pulled his companion back.

'Aw' hang yer hat up, Dave. We ain't got time ter waste on parlour games. Let's get the truth outa the *hombre* whar he's hidden them dollars.'

'Yeah, that's right.' Scaramouch joined him, then. Scaramouch didn't seem to fit in too well with these roughnecks; to Tombstone it seemed that he was nervous of them, especially doubtful about the man called Dave, the man who had posed as a marshal.

Dave growled, 'OK, Jan. But mebbe my time'll come when I c'n pay him back fer that piece o' work.' He stood and wiped his bloodied face with the back of his shirt sleeve.

Tombstone said, 'S'pose I tell you that I never took them dollars?'

Jan grinned and said, 'Nobody says you ever took 'em. But you got 'em.'

'S'pose I tell you I haven't got 'em?'

'Quit supposin'. You know whar they're hidden, don't you?'

Tombstone hesitated. It was only a fraction of a second, but it gave the show away.

Instantly Dave was back on the attack. He knew only one method of approach to any situation – the brutal way.

Tombstone was still half-lying against the wall. He saw Dave standing over him, saw the big roughneck's heavy boot drawn back, heard the fellar growl.

'He knows. Wal, he's goin' ter talk. He's goin' ter tell us whar it's hid, an' ef he's slow in findin' his tongue, he'll get my boot in his face!'

CHAPTER TWELVE

TOMBSTONE'S GOLDMINE

The boys watched Tombstone slide away into the darkness. In the distance was the swelling, threatening roar of the advancing mob, and the sky over the top of the rocky outcrop already seemed to be reddening with the light from the flaming torches that the horde carried.

A couple of minutes later Corny said, 'I'm goin' after the big fellar.' He swung off his horse.

Rip was startled. 'What about me?'

'Look, kid, jes' pull them hosses up the rock a bit, out o' sight of the trail an' grab some sleep.'

'With them galoots comin' up? You know they'd see me an' the hosses as easy as winkin' stickin' up thar.'

'Mebbe they won't come so far,' said Corny. 'Git them hosses up thar, in case someone comes a-ridin' through, an' jes' hope that Tombstone heads them galoots off.'

Rip wanted to argue. He was a young fire-eater, and he didn't like standing doing nothing while his companions went back to meet the danger.

Corny grinned in the darkness. 'You gotta stay while I go an' try an' help old Tombstone. I'm doin' no good hyar anyway.'

Before the kid had time to say anything to that, he had slipped away down the dark trail. He was just within sight of those tossing, blazing torches, when he heard shooting from the back of the crowd, and then someone yelling.

'Tombstone!' he thought, startled. That was Tombstone's voice all right. He started to run down the trail, and found others running with him, men coming in off their claims, unable to resist the excitement that the shooting created, back among the torch-lit mob.

He saw the advancing torch-bearers waver and then halt. And then there was a loud and rising excitement that travelled like a wave up the hillside to the west of the trail-more shooting. Instantly the line of torch bearers turned and started streaming up the hillside.

Corny stopped running so fast and grinned. The big fellar had created a diversion, but how he had done it, Corny couldn't guess. He thought, 'That Tombstone, he's as cunnin' as a cinnamon b'ar!'

He found other men running ahead of him, and that presented difficulties in the way of spotting his comrade. Suddenly his foot caught in something soft, and he went flying. He heard a groan as he hit the ground, and he rose quickly and went fumbling back.

There was someone stirring on the roadway, someone moving and cursing feebly. Corny got him by the shoulders and pulled him into a sitting position. But as soon as he felt the weight of the *hombre* he knew, even in the darkness, that it wasn't Tombstone. Tombstone was a bigger man than this. Corny felt relieved.

He said, 'What's the matter, pardner? What happened to you?'

The man groaned. 'Some galoot pulled me off my hoss an' beaned me. Ef I could lay my hands. . . .'

Suddenly the man found himself alone, talking to himself. Corny hadn't time to play nursemaid. His first thought when he heard the man's words was, 'Tombstone!' It could only be Tombstone who had pulled the fellar off his horse.

Corny's immediate thought was that Tombstone had secured the horse and gone riding quickly down the trail to get the mob riding after him. He started to run down the trail again.

Not more than a hundred yards ahead he heard horses' hoofs striking on the bare rock. He almost ran into the group of horsemen. Simultaneously he noticed one thing.

This party of horsemen were quietly, almost stealthily, leaving the scene of the disorder.

Suspicion came to him immediately – suspicion that these men might be the phoney marshal – for Corny had no doubts about that – and his 'posse'. Corny couldn't see that he could do any good following Tombstone, as he thought, up that hostile hillside, but it seemed to him that he might learn something if he followed these men for a while.

They weren't risking speed down that rocky trail, so he had no difficulty in keeping up with them. After a while he saw them approach a ramshackle hut on the outskirts of the little shanty town. Then a light flared . . . and he saw someone being dragged in, someone who looked uncommonly like Tombstone.

He crept close to the hut and walked round until he found a window. It was dirty, but he'd be able to see through it. He took off his hat, so that the wide brim wouldn't betray him, then cautiously rose on tip-toe and peered through the narrow window.

So it was that Corny was witness to the interrogation of the big cowboy – saw Tombstone strike back and send the 'marshal' reeling with his face cut open. Corny grinned. That was just like the big fellar. Even though he was bound hand and foot, he was still a man to be reckoned with.

Corny tried to hear what was being said, but the words came out to him in a subdued growl, so that only an occasional word was distinguishable. He badly wanted to hear, so he started to walk slowly around the hut trying to find some crack which might let the sound out. There were plenty of cracks, and he listened at them but always there was too much scuffling of feet, too many coughs and incidental noises for him to hear what was being said.

So he started to go back to the window. . . .

He stiffened, suddenly. He was sure that someone had moved across the way where another ramshackle dwelling stood. He halted in the shadows and waited, but no one moved across in those other deep shadows.

Corny had to make sure; he couldn't start up any rescue operations if there was some sentry or watcher outside, though he hadn't noticed anyone when he first came up.

He went down on all fours, to keep below the level of any light that came from the hut, and started to move around among the shadows, his idea being to come up on the other *hombre* from the side – if there was a *hombre*, that was.

Hardly daring to breathe, he moved slowly from one dark area to another. It took him several minutes to reach the other hut, but he felt that he hadn't made any betraying noise in doing so.

Pausing for a moment to listen, he quietly slipped out his gun. Another pause – this time he was sure that he heard some sound round the corner.

He stepped out quickly, crouching. . . .

No one was there.

Slowly he edged his way to the far corner. Turned it, gun ready. And again no one was there.

He made a complete circuit of the hut without seeing anyone. He paused, perplexed. Back of his mind was that uneasy prompting of instinct – 'There was someone there. He's gone now, but someone was there!'

It didn't make him any happier, standing in those shadows. But after a while he moved quietly across to the other hut again. He didn't know what had happened to Tombstone, but he had to try and get the big fellar free somehow.

Cautiously he raised his head to the window and looked in. He was in time to see the 'marshal' standing, boot poised, as if about to kick the fallen cowboy in the face.

That was enough for Corny. He wasn't going to stand by and see his pard hurt. Swiftly he came round to the door – raised his foot and shoved so hard he nearly crashed the flimsy door off its hinges. Then he jumped into the room, gun flaming.

One of the men had streaked for his gun as the boy came bursting in. Corny smashed his shoulder for him, and the man went screaming with pain on to his back against one of the bunks.

Corny shouted, 'Up with yer hands! One move an' I'll perforate you!'

From the floor Tombstone called, 'Good boy, Corny. Set one o' them galoots ter unfasten these ropes. Mebbe Scaramouch had better do it.'

That startled the boy, standing in the doorway with his gun ready. 'Scaramouch? He's hyar?' He hadn't expected that. It took him slightly off his guard.

'Watch out!' roared Tombstone. Someone had made a quick movement from the shadows of the lower bunk. It was where the sulking, nervous Scaramouch had been lurking.

Corny snarled and wheeled, his gun spraying lead. A gun blatted flame from the under the bunk, but the lead just sailed out harmlessly through the open door. Then Scaramouch came tumbling forward on to his face, his mouth working as if he were trying to say something but couldn't find the voice.

Slowly he went down, then suddenly he was dead. Corny had got him in the throat. Scaramouch had no need for the twelve thousand dollars where he was going.

Corny rapped, 'Mebbe that'll convince you I ain't in a playin' mood.'

Tombstone had levered himself upright against the wall. He called again, 'Make 'em drop their guns, and then set someone on ter untie me.' He didn't like being tied when there was a fight breaking out around him.

The boy waved his gun. 'You heard. Drop them guns – pronto!'

Someone came through the doorway and said, 'Drop your gun, pardner – pronto!'

Corny gasped as a gun barrel stabbed through his shirt in the middle of his back. Tombstone groaned with disappointment. So near – so near to release . . . so near to escape . . . so near to the goldmine he had discovered in the last fifteen minutes!

A rough-looking *hombre* had marched in behind him with a gun. There was blood on his forehead, and he looked in a mean mood.

Dave exclaimed, 'Bridgy! We thought you'd gone after them kids. You came jest in time, I reckon.'

'I sure did.' The man's eyes glittered. 'I didn't go after no kids. Someone pulled me off'n my hoss an' slugged me on the bean with a six-shooter, I reckon. When I find out who did it . . .' His gun jerked threateningly. Evidently he was a man who regarded a bang on the head as something very personal.

'I had ter walk back, an' I jes' got hyar in time ter see this galoot sneaking round by the window. He came after me, but I moved away. When he came in hyar, I jes' nacherly followed.'

'Good job you did,' growled one of the men looking down at the dead Scaramouch and the groaning *hombre* with the shattered shoulder. 'Guess thar wouldn't have bin many of us left in another five minutes, the rate this kid was goin' on.'

'Yeah, we got a few things ter settle with this kid,' growled Dave, and he moved slowly, threateningly, across to where Corny was standing with his hands raised above his head. Tombstone saw what was coming. Dave wouldn't be any gentler with the kid, because he was young. And Corny knew it, too.

Dave stopped, a yard away from the boy. His brutal, bearded face parted in a leer of sadistic satisfaction, then his fist came back to strike. . . .

Tombstone, bound though he was, wasn't altogether helpless. The thing was, the other men thought he was out of the reckoning. Suddenly he launched himself away from the wall, falling face downwards across the gun arm of the *hombre* standing behind Corny.

He heard the gun roar, heard the thud of the bullet in the board floor. Then he was blinded by the flame from the gun which scorched his eyebrows; there was the smell of burning gunpowder in his nostrils.

He went down, rolling so as to get under the feet of the startled gun-toter and bring him crashing down on top of him, and as he rolled he yelled, 'Hit the trail, Corny! Git away – you can't do any good hyar!' Then the gun-toter came crashing down on top of him and he found himself on the floor underneath a vicious hand-to-hand fight.

Corny's gun was on the floor, where he had dropped it when that gun stabbed into his back. Behind him, covering the door and so preventing the escape that Tombstone desired, were the rolling bodies of his pardner and the gun toter.

But there was something Corny could do, even if he couldn't get out of the hut. He could fight.

He started by kicking Dave slap in the middle of his stomach. It wasn't a nice thing to do, but there was no time for niceties. Anyway, Dave had been quite ready to kick his partner's head open. . . .

Dave seemed to rise on the point of the kid's boot and go back a couple of yards before he crashed on to a bunk, where he lay sprawled out and gasping for wind.

The other two men came in, arms flailing. They were at such close quarters that no one could use a gun even if they got at one.

Tombstone, rolling over, saw the kid fighting like a hellcat against two bigger, more powerful men – and dirty fighters. He saw Corny's fists jabbing out, for a minute holding the men off. Saw one of the men trying to swing a box and hit the kid, only the kid leapt to one side and it hit Dave instead and brought a bellow of pain from that *hombre*. Then the gun-toter rolled off the cowboy and jumped into the fight, both feet going. Corny caught one on the knee and gasped with pain. It slowed him. Instantly he was cornered, and a barrage of blows swung out and hammered him. Tombstone knew that he couldn't stand this for more than a few seconds. . . .

He looked round desperately, trying to see some way of helping the kid. He saw the oil lamp on top of the chest by the door. Round he squirmed on his back, then suddenly he lashed out with his feet and sent the chest toppling over.

For a second he thought that his plan had failed. True the hut was now in darkness, and that probably saved the kid from a lot of blows. But at that range they couldn't miss, not even in the dark. Tombstone heard a rough voice growl, 'Hold up, I got the kid. Get that light goin' while I hang on ter him.

And then there was an explosion of light in the place. The lamp had broken, the oil had run out across the floor, and now the dying flame from the wick had reached it and touched it off.

In a second the floor of the but seemed a raging inferno. Tombstone saw startled faces turn towards the red light. Saw the quick-witted Corny react instantly, lashing out and freeing himself and then come jumping across the flame patch to where the big cowboy lay.

Even as he was jumping, he saw Dave come staggering to his feet, his pain-racked face suddenly quickening to this new danger – of being burned alive. . . . Tombstone saw the *hombre* with the bust shoulder stagger screaming to his feet and come plunging headlong through the flames that now roared like a wall across the room.

Then Corny had stooped and grabbed his gun and stuck it back in its holster. And then he had hold of Tombstone, and the big cowboy found himself being dragged out into the cool night air.

Next minute the whole gang had come through the fiery doorway. They came out drawing their guns. Dave especially was going to have revenge for what had happened this night. His face was contorted with fury. He had expected an easy share of twelve thousand dollars; instead of which he had had his face bust open by a bound man, then his stomach nearly kicked off him by a kid, and now this hut – so valuable in these parts – was going up in flames. He didn't think that it was his own fault, that he had brought it on himself. At this moment he could only think of getting even with the two authors of his pain and disaster.

Corny saw the danger and tumbled Tombstone into a deep, dry, rain gully. As he fell in atop of the cowboy, lead spat over his head. Instantly he came round, his gun barking – twice, then the hammer clicked. He hurriedly reloaded.

Those first two shots scattered the four toughs, and they took cover. The hut flamed brilliantly, lighting up the gun battle almost as if it had been daylight. In the distance Corny could hear men shouting and running, as the fire and gun explosions attracted attention. But he guessed that no one would come and interfere ... in these parts gun duels were regarded as private, and a fellar just got on with his own business when one was in progress. Corny knew that he would have to fight this battle out alone.

Tombstone said, 'Hell, this ain't at all comfortable, kid. Get me outa these ropes.'

The kid said, 'You gotta wait until I get these *hombres'* heads down,' and he opened fire at the roughs across the firelit stretch in front of the blazing hut.

The heads went down. The kid reloaded and then swiftly cut through the big cowboy's bonds round his wrists. 'Help yourself,' he said, and shoved the knife into Tombstone's hands. Then he went back to work on the attackers.

Tombstone rose stiffly, saying, 'Ef I only had a gun,' then stooped swiftly as a bullet screamed over his head.

Corny called, 'They're closing in, Tombstone. Thar's a couple bang in front, an' another pair workin' round to our rear. Reckon this place is gonna get hot, soon.'

Desperately he tried to stay the pair from encircling them. His gun blatted hate, but they seemed to survive it. Every second or so here was a quick rush and the pair had moved a little farther round behind.

This rain gully was a trap now, with no way out except under fire from the other men's guns. Tombstone saw the lines of desperation on the kid's forehead. He knew they were in a tight spot this time. This gang had wanted them alive before for the information they thought they could give. Now they wanted them dead – because of the trouble they had caused.

No mistaking it, they were shooting to kill. And no mistaking it, they were in a commanding position now, on the edge of the circle of light. And they were closing in; all the time they were moving steadily closer. . . .

Corny suddenly sat back and howled like a coyote. Tombstone came wheeling round, startled. 'What's wrong, kid? You feelin' all right?'

Corny turned. The lines of desperation had faded. He grinned. 'Sure I'm all right. Didn't you hear what I heerd? I heerd a coyote howl out yonder. An' thar ain't no coyotes round these parts, I guess. So I reckon it's thet kid brother tryin' ter find me. He musta got tired o' waitin'. He won't need no tellin' after that yell that we're in the middle o' this gun battle. . . .'

Tombstone grabbed him. 'Listen!'

There was the drum of hoofs on the hard ground, approaching. Several horses.

'Could be Rip!' breathed Corny. 'Get ready, old timer.'

Tombstone shouted, 'Look out! They're rushin' us!' Corny whirled. Dave and other *hombre* were almost on top of them, guns blazing. They had suddenly jumped out from behind the building just back of the rain gully.

Then Tombstone saw the other pair jumping in – even

the man with the shattered shoulder was walking steadily forward, gun spraying flame and lead.

All in one second there was deadly hail all around them, forcing them down ... a leaden curtain of death that defied them to lift their heads even to defend themselves. And the *hombres* were coming nearer. ...

A rider streaked into the fireglow, almost flat on his horse's back. Alongside ran two riderless horses. It was Rip. His gun roared and the bearded Dave suddenly crumpled and fell into the rain gully. Tombstone, quick as lightning, picked up his four-five.

Rip fired again, and the *hombre* with the shattered shoulder took another pill and it didn't do him any good. The other three roughs turned and streaked back for cover.

Tombstone and the kid came jumping out, guns roaring after the fleeing trio.

'Up!' bellowed Rip. 'Git movin' or they'll open up on us from behind that hut!'

He didn't pause. Rip knew they had only seconds before the gunmen again got the whip hand ... in five more seconds they'd be behind cover, and then, at that short range, they couldn't miss.

Rip kept the horses running so as to save seconds. Tombstone and Corny sheathed guns and dived for harness as their frightened mounts crashed by. They mounted them at top speed, with a quick rolling jump. They were flat down on their horses' backs and out into the darkness before the first gun opened up again.

They slept that night on a strand by the edge of the sea, with their fire sparkling from the slow-moving waves. But before they slept, Tombstone took out paper and pencil and laboriously wrote by the light of the fire.

That made the kids curious. It was the first letter they

had ever seen their pardner write.

'Say, *hombre*, what're you up to?' demanded Rip suspiciously. 'You seem in an all-fired good mood ternight. I don't know why. With all Sacramento rememberin' us as claim-jumpers, that puts an end to our hopes of strikin' gold in these hyar hills.'

Corny said, 'So what? Reckon we'd never have found any, anyway. An' I wouldn't want ter be a miner, at that.'

Rip said, 'But the big fellar wanted ter make enough money ter be able ter set up ranch fer him an' Belle. He should be disappointed.'

Tombstone finished. 'I ain't disappointed at all.' he said calmly. 'I know whar there is a gold mine.'

The kids came out of their blankets at that. 'You know? Where? What's that letter you bin writin'?'

Tombstone smiled. 'I jes' wrote ter Belle, tellin' her I wouldn't be seen' her fer mebbe four or five months. But I told her ter start lookin fer a nice li'l ranch fer her an' me.'

Then he sat up. 'I learned something ternight. I learned that Dutch Maxie got killed a few weeks back. He left no heirs an' everyone jes' grabbed what they could. That means that ef we find them twelve thousand dollars he lost, we have a good claim to 'em.'

'Yeah, but we don't know whar they are?' said Rip.

'I got a good idea,' drawled Tombstone. 'I got an idea them dollars is jes' back o' the Mexican *cantina* outside Santa Fe.'

'What?' gasped the boys.

Tombstone said, 'Sheddup, ef you want ter hear. Scaramouch was with that gang back in that hut. Now think about Scaramouch. He left Dutch Maxie's the day before the robbery. But mebbe he sneaked back in the night an' stole them bills. He didn't have no saddle, so he took yours. . . .'

The kids began to see it, now.

'Remember how someone ripped our saddles ter bits when we got into 'Frisco yesterday. Remember how Scaramouch hugged that old saddle of Corny's so carefully – he even took it into the *cantina* that day we met up with him in Santa Fe. Remember we were surprised at the fuss he kicked up when we took it off'n him?

'Well, I guess he'd hidden the twelve thousand dollars inside the saddle!'

'Holy smoke!' said Corny. 'So ef we c'n find that saddle, we get four thousand dollars apiece. An' I know whar it is. You slung it at Jep Shaker, Rip, an' he jes' threw it among them prickly pears. No one goes picnicking among prickly pears, so I guess that old saddle will still be thar.'

Rip was on his feet.

'Where are you goin'?' demanded Corny.

'I'm gonna set off right now an' find that saddle. Jest in case someone does decide ter look among them prickly pears.'

Tombstone said, 'It'll be thar, kid. Grab some sleep.' And he turned over comfortably on his blanket, to dream of Belle and the lovely ranch that four thousand dollars would bring.

And the saddle *was* there, with the dollar bills sewn neatly inside. . . .